Epigraph

"To have great pain is to have certainty. To hear that another person has pain is to have doubt."

- The Body in Pain by Elaine Scarry

Life of Trees

Prologue

There is something mysteriously captivating about a bare, lifeless tree in the winter. There it stands - as tall as it has ever been - holding the countless branches it has grown over the years. There is something about succumbing to our emotions when looking upon and realizing the beauty that is still left that has a way of opening our eyes to the comparison it draws to our personal life. That very thought will make you reminisce. You think to yourself of the memories you've made throughout the years and the lessons you've learned. You think on the things that have turned you into the individual that you have become. The highs. The lows. Cheers. Tears. All of it.

Take a moment to think of the life of a tree and you will realize that as people we aren't much different. The way we age, is our way of growing taller. The people we meet, relationships we build, the moments we make, our entire life story are the branches that expand from our tree. This shapes us, reveals us. Now the leaves... the leaves are just simply the expression of our happiness. They fill our branches, showcasing an amazing image (if we make it so). Over time, just as the seasons throughout the year, we are faced with the peaks and valleys of life.

We go through the joys of Spring and Summer. During these seasons the leaves are bright and green. That time when everything seems to be right. Everything falls into its place and smiles are the norm.

Then comes Autumn. The weather begins to mildly change. Troubles may arise but we get through them because we find places to draw strength. We overcome them through the happiness we have already gathered and occasionally even gain more happiness throughout the season. The constant highs and lows affect us but don't break us. So the leaves change colors. This season takes its time molding us, but in the end it leaves us uniquely gorgeous.

Then we endure our Winter. Our lowest moments. They seemingly leave us cold, dark, empty, and sorrowful. The season where leaves fall from the tree. Sadly, this is the season where for some trees, all of the leaves wither away. The same can be said for human happiness. Sometimes the battles of winter become too much, and all the leaves, all of the happiness, slowly vanish. Some trees, never gain another leaf. Some people, never find happiness again.

Now after this season there is left a genuinely beautiful image. Only leaving a collage of memories, relationships, and life. The same as the leafless tree, if we can make it through the seasons, life comes full circle. That is the beauty of it all. To experience each season is to experience life.

Except what about the ones who only experience winter, yet are forced to live out the other seasons as if they get the same euphoria as anyone else? Some get overwhelmed in the snowstorms. Others are so accustomed to the pain that they find peace in the cold nature. Some scream out to experience another season, but no one can hear their cries. Hasn't it always been said that "If a tree falls in the forest, and nobody is around to hear it, does it make a sound?" It's ok though. Who needs leaves anyway?

Chapter 1: James

"James wake up. Hey. It's time to wake up," he says as he shakes my body to break my sleep. "You've gotta get up. Big day ahead."

I awake and rub my fingers over my eyes. I take a deep yawn while arching my back with outstretched arms for the best morning stretch imaginable.

"James, come on let's go. Get up buddy," he said while standing bed side.

I finally take the time to open my eyes and I see the largest smile in the world. In a combination of utter disbelief and happiness, I mutter the words "Good morning Dad."

"Good morning son. I love you."

With tears beginning to form from my eyes I hold them back just long enough to say "I love you too dad!"

The alarm sounds 5:45 a.m.

I roll over and sporadically move my hands along the bed to find my phone in order to put an end to the constant ringing in my ear. I end the alarm and motion to my left.

"Hey Dad can we go t...." I start to scream until my disappointment silences me.

At that moment reality set in. It was just a dream. My dad was never there to wake me up. He hasn't been there to do that since before his untimely death on February 12, 2014. Today is September 6, 2017 and my father, my best friend, is never coming back. At least not for real anyway. Over three and a half years have come and gone, yet there has been one constant. Dreams are far better than reality. I can't feel pain while I'm asleep.

All I wanted was to sleep until I could awaken and feel like I had regained some of the time I had lost with him. Whether they were real or simply dreams, it didn't matter to me. As long as it could be remembered, they would forever be engraved in my mind as memories. But just a normal nap wasn't enough time. Although inducing sleep wasn't a problem for me. Over the course of three plus years in dealing with grief, I taught myself a few things. Lucky me. I turned to my side then curled myself into a ball underneath the blankets and whisper to myself "It's time to go."

After fumbling through the junk I had stashed inside the drawers of my night stand, I found them. The remainder of my prescription for muscle relaxants I received weeks earlier. I grabbed the entire bottle then walked in the kitchen and grabbed my magnum bottle of moscato. With all I needed in hand I slowly stepped into the bathroom. With warm water filling the bathtub, my thoughts ran wild. My fear of not knowing if I should move forward with this, combined with the eagerness to see my father's face, along with my desire to briefly live the life that I so desperately wanted with everyone I cared for involved, was more than enough to haunt my mind. But all of those thoughts immediately vanished when I stepped foot in the tub.

Completely clothed, I edge my body in until I am almost fully submerged in the water. I open the moscato and grab two pills. I pop the pills and the drinking commenced. Here I am thinking that drinking a one and a half liter bottle of wine would take me a while to consume. Quickly I realized that when you're drowning out the noise that is your mind, you tend to move faster. Four minutes pass, and half the bottle is gone. The room is spinning. Everything begins to blur. Time to put down three more pills. I chase the pills with more wine. What happens next? Euphoria. Pure bliss swept over my body as the high kicked in from the drugs in my body. I paused to soak in the feeling. I drink another fifth of the bottle then take two more pills. Time stands still. I decide to take a half of one last pill and finish off the wine. My heart begins to race as the lightheadedness intensifies. I can't breath. What had I done? This isn't how it was supposed to happen. I am now petrified.

Then suddenly, it was as if the nerves in my body completely shut off altogether. My limp body grows cold with chills covering my skin as my eyes roll back and my hand falls down the side of the tub into the water. A million memories rush to my brain in the matter of seconds. Finally, I take a deep breath.

One deep inhale to fill my lungs up with as much air as they could hold. Then an long extended exhale that released all of my energy along with the air in my body, leaving nothing to give.

At the end of the breath, the regret sets in. A deafening silence fills the room and my heavy eyes leisurely begin to close.

The alarm sounds once more, now at 6:30 a.m. This time to no answer.

Chapter 2: Miranda

Dear Miranda,

Have you ever wanted to be with someone so much, that you don't care to get a message from ANYONE else? Every time your phone goes off, you only desire to see one name. That's what happens with me. You're the only one I feel like talking to. And you're the only one I want to be with. I know you've asked why I like you. So let me just tell you each reason in the order it came.

Now I would be lying to you if I said I didn't message you from the start because you were this beautiful girl who I had no idea who she was. All I knew was that I had to know you. From the first conversation we had, it began. At first, I had this ongoing curiosity of if you even wanted to talk to me at all. You were being fairly short, no lol or haha and no emojis. You just answered whatever question and I had and that was it. But something told me to talk to you until you said to stop. Now I'm glad I did. Because after you finally broke through with "my family drives me crazy sometimes," and we started getting further into the conversation, you started to become someone who I wanted to talk to more and more.

The first talk we had wasn't about anything deep, or heart warming, just normal talk. But I remember how happy you made me from that moment. The way it had become so stimulating just from seeing your name. Then the next few days came and we talked more. I started learning more things about you - the way you feel, the way you think. I began slowly, piece by piece, thinking of you and I together. You were exactly the girl I wanted to be with. That happiness you brought me, followed by the thoughts of you and me together, pushed me closer to you with every other message. Every heart eyes, every kiss, every heart, every smile, was sent as genuine and honest as they could possibly be. Fast forward to the wonderful night where I first met you. You swore you looked terrible but I saw the most beautiful girl on the face of the Earth.

You see, you already had me from "hello." Then the second I looked into those amazing, breathtaking eyes and saw your captivating and ridiculously pretty smile, that is moment where everything else ceased to exist. Nothing mattered to me. No one else mattered. The only thing I was concerned with, was laying my eyes on you, recognizing that I was looking at the girl I wanted over everyone else. The girl who I would and will choose over anyone on this Earth. That's a moment I'll never forget.

Then after that we got to talk some more. I got to learn about how you had been hurt, from your undeniably crazy ex and the insane ones who cheated on you. While I was listening to how bad your exes had messed up things between you two, all I could think of was "Thank you for leading her here to me." Because I want to be with you more than anything. I know that's probably scary, but it's true. I can promise you every day that I won't ever hurt you, but I know I just have to show you instead. I'm willing to do that.

Unfortunately, I thought everything was going to be ruined by the random rumors that were spread about me from people i don't even know. He's this. He's that. Womanizer. Prick. Best of all, a hoe. Then I noticed how calm you were and seemingly unphased you were by it. Even laughing at it. That completed it. We talked about it and I couldn't believe how understanding you were. Because Lord knows I was scared they had ended something before it could be the best thing that ever happened to me. I'm glad it didn't.

Now take us to the night where we first got to spend time together. It was fantastic. In every sense of the word. From the laughs at jokes we made, at you being SO INDECISIVE :) from the pictures on your wall. Watching movies and shows, talking, then looking back at the tv and barely knowing what's going on.....Our first kiss with each other to our last kiss of the night. Accidentally falling asleep together. All of it. It was the best night. It was something that I didn't want to end.

I like you for the person you are, the way you've made me feel, the happiness you bring me, the honesty you give and you crave, for the heart you're so hesitant to give to me. You, all of you, I like it all. I like the time I spend with you, I like the way we joke and laugh. I like the thoughts of having you in my life. I love calling you mine, and I love being yours.

Baby, I know you've been hurt before. I've had my share of heartbreaks, not even all from relationships. I've been broken to the lowest point someone could go. And now I know that that feeling isn't ever coming back. I'm long long over it but I know you make me happier than anything in this world. I want to do nothing but return that happiness. I will NEVER, EVER hurt you. I know that this distance is a killer and it seems like the literal worst case scenario for us (which it probably is) but I can assure you that I'm the end it will be worth it if we make it through. I want to make it passed anything because I want all of this with you. I want to make you smile uncontrollably when you're walking around and talking to me. I want your heart to warm when I kiss you. I want you to feel safe and secure when I hold you. I want you to know that I hold you above everyone else. I want you to know that you are my girl. For as long as your heart desires. I Love You Miranda Walker.

Forever Yours,
Brad

"Hurry home to me," I murmur while clinching the letter to my chest. I put it down on the table and take a sip of my now lukewarm coffee. I rush upstairs to burst into my room. Christmas lights and pictures fill every corner. A turquoise tint to the light illuminates the room from my overdose of the color caused by the comforter set and curtains.

I walk around my bedroom, staring at the picture of Brad and I on the wall and reminisce. In an instant, I start to sulk in the thought of how much I miss him. Then something completely freezes me. A single picture that totally embodied the feeling of embrace that I so longed for.

I remember his mother taking this picture for us. It was the picture of Brad and I from the night before he left to be stationed in San Antonio, Texas for the United States Air Force. He held me so tightly that it was like nothing I had ever felt before. So safe. So secure. So cherished. He held me as if to say "I'm never going to let you go." We looked at each other with pure bliss in our eyes. I was so happy to be in Brad's arms, but even more terrified of the fact that I had no idea when I would have that feeling again. He caressed my face and said "No matter the distance, I'll always be with you. Wherever you go, my love will follow." Then Brad leaned in slowly and kissed me. At that very moment I realized two things: that I was going to miss the hell out of him, and that I was absolutely in love with him.

"Smile," Brad's mom yelled.

To be honest, it's truly not the simple satisfaction of being in love that captivates me so much. But rather spending life with that special person. Having them be right there by your side and enjoying the incredible journey you two take along the way. Companionship. Isn't that what we all want?

Days like this, my skeptical mind runs rampant. I say "days like this," but with him I'm actually meaning every day. The reality that one can be loved and be in love to this magnitude seems so superficial. How is it possible to sustain such love when the two of us lie our heads down over a thousand miles apart?

I feel like I'm not alone when I say that it's such a comforting feeling in knowing that you have someone to shield you from the sheer nothingness that is being all alone. Sadly that shield is pretty nonexistent when that person is never actually there to hold it up. I am so unequivocally loved. So why is it that when he isn't here, I feel so alone?

Chapter 3: Dawson

It is 7:20 a.m. at Coastal County High School. A mass of students fill the hallways while a portion of them walk into the auditorium. By the second it becomes increasingly harder for me to breathe. I tap my fingers to the rhythm of *Hills and Valleys* by Tauren Wells while it plays softly in the background. Humming along to the song I quickly stop as I realized humming only made my breathing worsen. As the clock inches closer to 7:30, everyone takes their seat.

"Dawson, feel free to start whenever you're ready," Pastor Montgomery noted.

I nod my head as I wipe my sweaty palms on the side of my jeans meanwhile slowing my breathing to calm my nerves. My back starts to tingle and stiffen as I try to stretch it out to no avail. The tingling increased and soon I felt a weakness in my legs. After a few more useless stretches I shook them out to wake my body up. Volleyball apparently was taking its toll.

I look up to see countless faces - both known and unknown. "Lord be with me," I whisper.

"By show of hands, how many of you here have ever felt abandoned by God?" I asked. The hands of each and every individual in attendance to today's Fellowship of Christian Athletes meeting rose in the air. "Now how many of you have you stopped to ask yourself the question 'Did God forsaken me, or did I walk away from Him?'" I look out into the crowd to see everyone's arms either folded or propped on the arm rest of the school auditorium seats. I smirked at the sight. Not because I thought it was funny or anything, but because I expected it and I understood.

"What is it about that question that we seem to struggle with so much? Is it our sense of emotional suppression? That since we are the ones in pain, or have become negligent in our responsibilities, that it is our problem to face alone? We don't want to spread our sadness and negative energy any farther than our own self-conscious. ' I'm better off alone in this' we say to ourselves. Subconsciously we scream for help, but we dare not ask that favor of anyone. So as a result we unwillingly push everyone away. Everyone, including God. But why? Friends may come and go, but the Lord is forever."

The passion in my voice rose the more I spoke. Once sweaty palms now vice gripped the microphone as I paced back and forth on the stage.

"Why push forever away? When we look into Deuteronomy 31:6 it tells us 'Be strong and courageous. Do not be in dread of them, for it is the Lord your God who goes with you. He will never leave you or forsake you.' It's so unfortunate that we wallow in our sufferings to the degree that we blind ourselves from seeing God sitting right beside us. We numb ourselves from feeling his arms of protection around us. So we think we are alone. In reality, we were never alone and we will never be alone. Isaiah 30:18 says 'Therefore the Lord waits to be gracious to you, and therefore he exalts himself to show mercy to you. For the Lord is a God of justice; blessed are all those who wait for him.' In other words God is right there waiting. We want God to come straightforward to us but the Lord God is a gentleman who will not press Himself upon us unwillingly. Instead He waits for us to turn to Him in order for us to receive all of the compassion and love that has been awaiting us amidst the darkness. Once you turn your heart over to God you will find that his love is unquestioned and unmatched. He can give you all of the happiness your heart desires, but you have to give him your heart first in order for him to do it. I promise it's worth it. As I close today I want to challenge anyone out there facing demons in their life to be honest with themselves and ask 'Have I turned away from God?' Ask yourself because I promise you that even if you walked away from Him, He hasn't left you. He's still there waiting for you with open arms. No matter what you are going through, always remember these words I am about to say. I want you to engrain them in your heart and mind. "

I paused for a second to make sure I had the attention of everyone in the auditorium during that time. I took a few breaths to calm me down from the intensity I was speaking from and finally said, "You are loved. You are cherished. You are valuable. Most importantly you are never EVER alone. God Bless you all."

Chapter 4: Maddux

"Remember we're going to be out of town for the rest of the week and weekend for a business trip in Atlanta so don't do anything crazy. I want my house looking exactly how I left it," my mom said while she folded clothes and started to put them in she and dad's suitcases. "I don't really care if you have friends over or something but you better not go overboard. All chores are to be done. You need to ta.."

"Take care of the dogs, do homework, clean my room," I interrupted while numbering the list with my fingers sarcastically. "I got it mom you don't have to give me the same speech. It's alright."

Glaring almost through my soul from the annoyance caused from hearing my interruption, my dad walked into the room. "Shut your mouth and just listen to what she's saying!"

I nonchalantly rolled my eyes while turning my face away to the bedroom window so that they couldn't see it. Knowing that he would potentially spin my head around like something from the Looney Tunes if he caught me. Returning my focus to them, I stood there faking my attentiveness to their words, not caring to be lectured this early in the morning, especially before school. "Yes ma'am...No ma'am...Okay... I will...Yes ma'am," I repeated like a tape recorder as I impatiently awaited for the lecture to end.

"One last thing" my dad said. "I know it's your senior year of high school and there's going to be a lot of things going on. People are going to want to go out and do things they probably shouldn't do. Drink, party, and then get that fake senioritis trash, all of it. So it's all good to have fun and stuff and enjoy it but you need to make sure not to lose focus. Other kids are going to do whatever they may, but just remember that you don't have to be anyone but yourself." My parents leaned in for an incredibly awkward group hug, kissed me on the forehead, told me they loved me, then immediately kicked me out of the room.

Traditionally parents would give their children that cute speech before the first day of school. Obviously my parents are not what you would consider traditional. It's day three of school and now they decide to do it? Though it was a nice little talk, a few words stood out to me. You don't have to be anyone but yourself. Walking to my room to get ready for the day I imagined a scenario where I followed up my dad's statement with the words "Well I don't really know how to be 'myself'" while adding air quotes. "So I'm not sure what you want me to do about that so I'll just do what I've been doing."

As good of a reply as that might have been, the words reigned true. I didn't know how to be myself yet. Truthfully, being like others was kind of my way of figuring that out. On the surface, the joy certain things bring me has a way of drawing me out of my shell and slowly making me believe that I can actually start to piece together the puzzle that I am. Internally, the person I truly am and am meant to be sits imprisoned, desolate within the four walls of my psyche, desperately awaiting to reveal himself to me and the world. To be known, to be recognized for more than just my name, and to just find answer to the questions encircling my mind is really all I ask. You see when I say "to be known," I mean to be understood. Anyone in the world can know your name, where you live, even list friends of yours, but how many of those people actually understand you? How many understand the person you are, your character, your flaws, ambitions, who you are and who you want to be? Although it's hard to fathom being known by others when I struggle to know my own self.

Each and everyday I wake up with the exact same question yearning to be answered as I stare at my reflection in the mirror. Who am I? Where do I fit in and what role do I play in this strange thing called life? What is your purpose Maddux?

Unfortunately, each day I ask myself those questions as the sun rises, and my identity as a person just seems to fade along with the sunset, still unknown. Sometimes I have moments that lead me to think "This is what I am. This is me." The only problem with that thought is that it comes all too frequently, and withers away just as quickly. It is as if it only takes but the slightest of attraction to inspire me to venture into it. I have to almost try to become that person to see if it truly fits me.

Like the insane time I binged watched Generation Iron One and Two, The Perfect Physique and damn near any fitness video I could click on. The aspiration to become this fitness legend in the public eye was so appraise that I practically begged my parents for a weight set and gym membership. It was the best thing in the world. I loved every single moment. Well, for about a month and then I realized I hated to diet so much that it drove me crazy. I started to look at our chef when it was time to eat and then stare at the food. "Please! No more bland chicken breast. Give me a burger, with bacon, and fries, and a shake!" I would scream as I mentally checked this venture of my life up to trial and error. On the bright side, after a month, I thought I looked great.

There is one benefit of trying to find my way in the world. I've met a ton of people along the way. While it takes a lot for me to consider ones friends, my list of acquired acquaintances was virtually endless. I never completely found myself when meeting them all, but I did realize that my trial and error journey led people to see me as this extravert of a person. Oddly enough, through all of my self doubt, an extrovert was exactly what I was. Each of them played a part in me putting that small piece of the puzzle together, so what better way to mold more of the puzzle than to embrace that part of me? I've got the place entirely to myself for the weekend. My parents won't be back until late Sunday night. Why not bring everyone I know (and don't know) all together and add a few more for a night by hosting the greatest house party in this town's history?

Before the thought even had a chance of developing anymore I had already taken my phone out and instantly went to every form of social media and began to click on every name I recognized, being overly cautious to not accidentally click on a family member's name. Over a couple hundred names filled the list as I read them off to myself. After receiving my "Party at 1226 Summerlake Drive this Friday. Hosted by Maddux McDaniel" message, each person on the list only had one job to do for me: bring a friend. In the matter of ten minutes, I had it all set in motion. It took about thirty seconds before the "I'll be there" and "Is it alright if I bring some people" texts started invading my phone nonstop. This was reality now, and in my mind, after you invite well over two hundred people, each of whom is bringing someone, there was absolutely no turning back. No matter what. The first weekend of the school year and I have now taken it upon myself to make sure that all three thousand five hundred square feet of this house is filled with people and alcohol. One legendary night, never to be forgotten. Maddux McDaniel, will forever be known. It's worth the shot. I mean there are really only two possible outcomes. Either I find out more of myself and who I am, or I lose myself even more within the crowd of people. When there's somehow option C. My biggest fear of it all: to leave it all - what ever the result - at the end of the night and at the bottom of a bottle. Lucky for me, I really don't even drink much at all.

Chapter 5: James

Thrusting my hand above the water to clasp the side of the tub, I propelled my insensible body forward. Hyperventilating and wildly frightened, I sat there with water pouring down from the crown of my head and my drenched shirt. Water flowed down the outline of my face, dripping from my eyelashes while I examined every corner of the room dazed and confused. It may have been the perplexity I was feeling at the time, but my simple teenage instinct took over and suddenly I only wanted to do one thing. Find my phone.

Out of pure laziness I reach my arm outside of the bath onto the floor. I fish my hand around, knocking over the empty wine bottle and sliding the bottle of pills across the tile floor, until I feel my phone pressed against the wall. I dry my hand on the shower mat before grabbing my phone. That annoying tone of Siri popped up. "Siri get the hell off of my phone so I can see what time it is," I said.

"I'm sorry I didn't quite catch that," Siri responded.

"Of course you didn't."

The time showed 7:00 a.m. For some reason I panicked and jumped up to grab my toothbrush and scrubbed my teeth as if I was on a timer. I turned around and tried to quickly get back to the tub to drain the water. A little too quickly. One wrong step and my foot slid across the floor from the puddle of water I brought along with me. Before I knew it, my feet were above my head and I was looking at the ceiling. Then it dawned on me that I had no reason to be rushing. My house was four miles away from the school. I soon stood back up and drained the bathtub and turned the shower on. Standing there looking like I had just stepped out of a swimming pool, I undressed and as unmotivated as possible, got ready for my day.

School didn't start until eight and after getting dressed and grabbing my things I had forty-five minutes before I had to be at that place. A place that five days a week I dreaded to attend. Why? Because for seven hours a day, I put my emotional mask on and pretended that my life was this abundance of joy. No one likes a Debbie Downer, and I refused to be one. Though to my surprise, I decided that I would make my glorious appearance at Coastal County High School just a little bit early today.

I walked to the kitchen and looked for some food to eat before heading out. Fortunate for myself, my mom (whom had left hours earlier for work) had left a bacon egg and cheese biscuit behind in the refrigerator. Now I knew it probably wasn't for me and that by eating it I was surely doomed to be lectured about eating her food later that day, even though we both knew she likely had no intention to eat it herself. I could make something to eat, but that meant I was stuck in the house for a bit longer. "To be lectured or to leave it?," I questioned. I motioned my hands like a scale and of course the side for "eat the biscuit" won easily. I snatched the biscuit and made my way out of the house.

Upon arriving at school I sat in my car wondering why the hell I decided to be the one kid who chose to show up early. I don't even like school. Unfortunately I had already made the stupid decision to come. I walked in and scanned the lobby to think of my next move. Instantaneously there was a massive influx of students rushing in the same direction. Honestly my initial thought was that a fight had broken out. Then I figured that due to the lack of raised cell phones and camera flashes that it wasn't very probable. I followed the crowd to an apparent event the school was holding. I took my seat in the back of the room as it seemed to be starting.

Over the course of the next thirty seconds it became very clear why I was at school so early. Because without showing up prematurely, I never would've seen her stroll across that stage in her white cable-knit sweater; maroon infinity scarf draped over her neck with blue skinny jeans and tan UGG boots to match. The lights highlighting the way her impressively wavy auburn hair flowed down to the middle of her back.

She walked behind the podium on stage, seeming to be a bit worried as she looked out into her audience. Then suddenly a group of over sixty students went mute. The result of the silence was one of those "Life pressed pause" situations you always read in books or see in movies. She looked out in the crowd one more time and spoke. Now the things she said isn't what I would normally spend time trying to understand, but her words were awe-inspiring. Just the attention her beauty demanded made it interesting, but the message she spoke, the clear rigidity it possessed, made it mesmerizing.

Before I knew it the first bell sounded and I leisurely made my way to Mrs. Campbell's for Pre-Calculas. Who's bright idea was it to make teens think of math so damn early in the morning? To that person, please know I despise you. Although I will say that as much as I disliked math, Mrs. Campbell was my favorite teacher; so that evened things out. I walked passed the endless bodies of underclassmen sprinting to find their classrooms. It was the third day of my senior year and the fear of being late to class was hilarious to me because I remember when that was me, yet aggravating because someone seemed to bump into me every three steps I took. Thankfully, I made it around the corner and took my seat into Mrs. Campbell's class. Listening to my classmates chatting about their adventures and the pleasurable chaos that was the 2017 summer, I accidentally spoke aloud. "Hmm, must be nice."

"Damn right it is," said Wyatt.

Wyatt has been my best friend since the sixth grade. Surprisingly we had been bitter enemies of one another just the year before. Well, at least he was my enemy. I didn't like him at all. Not because I thought he was bad guy or anything; honestly I

didn't even know him. It just so happened he played for our rival.
I'm not sure if I even believed that was a good reason to dislike
someone, but it felt right at the time. My dad was my coach and to
be straightforward, we ran our city when it came to baseball. The
same was said about Wyatt and his dad's team. We played each
other a few times a year and championships were only to be
decided between us. We were the youth comparison of Yankees -
Red Sox. Then - and to this day I don't know who was responsible
- we decided to merge the best from our teams. With both of our
dads as coaches, and being on one of the most dominant 13-15
year old teams ever, and after realizing we were pretty much the
same, it's needless to say we quickly became friends. We went
from being on fields holding bats to being in fields holding beer.
That's the kind of friendships baseball creates I guess. The rest is
history.

Wyatt then patted me on the back, looking anxious about
something.

"Bro I know you heard about to the party at Maddux's house
on Friday night after the game. First one of the year. Apparently
shit is supposed to be nice. You trying to go party?," he asked.

"Really?," I said with a laugh. "Come on, you know me better
than to ask that." Which he did. Being the fact that I was
notoriously known for my everlasting appearances at parties. I
think I can count on one hand how many parties my friends and I
have missed since freshman year. With all of them being from
freshman year. Partying actually became one of the few fun things

I had. The socializing aspect though, not always the getting drunk part. Luckily, I was the fun kind of drunk. You know the type who is always at the center of everyone's Snapchat stories. Not the obnoxious kind who can't handle their liquor and decides to occupy the bathroom for an hour continuously throwing up; or worse, the one - who as soon as they get a little liquor in them - thinks they can beat up everyone at the party. In retrospect it didn't take much partying to find out that the hangover after you've gotten drunk is terrible. On the contrary, the feeling you have while getting drunk with all of your friends knowing there will be story to tell for the next week of school...priceless.

"Yes that's true" Wyatt laughed. "You wanna just ride with me over there? We'll just stop by and grab a few beer. There's supposedly going to be a load of alcohol there anyway. I don't know how true it is, but I'm not going to take the chance of possibly being the only ones without something to drink."

"Alright yea that's fine. Just let me know when you wanna head out" I replied simultaneously thinking of what beer I wanted to buy.

"Bet that works. We'll probably be leaving closer to ten."

"Got it."

The commotion of the classroom slowly diluted. We turned our attention to the board to see Mrs. Campbell writing out some quadratic equation. "Find the vertex" she said surely knowing that half of the class had no idea what was going on. She tapped the board with her marker in annoyance with "it's going to be a long day" expressed all throughout her body language. I felt bad for her. It was like the inattentiveness of her students slowly drained her by the seconds. She was an amazing teacher. She could at least get some attention. I found it awkward to be thinking that when I was typically one of the people who weren't paying attention.

In the minutes that followed I finally answered the equation. I put my pencil down and stared at my paper. The vertex is two - twelve. "Dad's birthday. Also his death day" I thought. Slowly my mind ravaged with grief. "Wow. Two- twelve? Really? February 12th you never cease to dissatisfy me" I said to myself. The demons that are the spiraling thoughts of my psyche began to wear me down by making their opinions heard deep within my conscious. "Two - twelve. Those numbers familiar? You see your began on this amazing uphill slope. You're happy. Your family is whole. School is amazing. You have this radiating confidence. You're just so sure of everything. Cute. February 12th, it all peaks. It stops. That precious life that you USED to have, is now no more. Everything stopped for you that day and it all changed. Cue the commencement of your spiraling downfall. Only instead of a slow winding spiral down, you saved yourself the rollercoaster and just went out a bit, still sinking, then all at once plummeted straight down. Smart boy. Now look at you. Kudos for not being contagious with it. Its for the best you know? I mean you're taking pills at six in the morning to escape. Come On. Escape what? Reality? Your thoughts? No no no no no! I admire you though for refusing to hit rock bottom. However, how far can you fall?

There's no parachutes on this free fall. Til death do us part big man."

Moments later I snap out of this transparency to see that I'm the only one still seated. Everyone was grabbing their stuff and walking out. Mrs. Campbell, ranting on about things we should know and the homework assignment for the night. What the hell happened? Class literally just started. I answered the equation like five minutes ago. Right? I cautiously grab my things, looking and feeling confused and lost. How does fifty minutes just pass by? Then it dawned on me. What happened was that in an instance, the thoughts had all flooded my mind. I sat there in my seat, motionless. My body was there in the classroom but my mind had ripped me out of the room and sucked me into this damning space, floating in pain, while I was courageously fighting to get out. The gears of my mind winded down, helping me realize this wasn't the most graceful description but then again I'm pretty sure there's no other way to put it without lying to myself. Thankfully I had six more hours in my school day to forget about it all.

Walking back to my locker I look around staring at the blue devil logo that seemed to cover every corner of the school. I continued down the hall with my head looking anywhere but right in front of me until I felt the end of a binder stab into my ribs. I tried to stop myself but being hit in the face by hair as she put her head down only made it worse. Then suddenly the binder to the ribs was the least of my pain as the binder and a textbook fell on to my toes.

"I'm sorry. I wasn't looking" I said trying to pick up the loose paper from the binder.

"It's ok. I'm just a teacher's assistant this period so it doesn't really matter" she joked.

Her voice was soft, and all too familiar. Taking a second to see who she was I motioned my head up. To my surprise, it was her.

"Umm I don't think we've ever really met. I'm James...James Taylor. I think I saw you earlier?" I mumbled out of sheer nervousness.

Now I'm no believer in fate or love at first sight or anything, but the chances of me seeing her on the first day I actually decide to show up early, now being frozen by the gaze in her hazel eyes, sure is starting to change my mind on that.

"Nice to meet you" she smiled. "I'm not sure. Were you at FCA earlier?"

"Yea I was. It was great. You were great. Today was actually the first time I've ever gone."

"Thank you. I'm glad you liked it. You should come more."

"I will" I murmured, standing up to hand her back the binder.

"Thanks again. Oh and umm, I'm Dawson."

Chapter 6: Dawson

Five minutes later and the ringing of the tardy bell resonated throughout the school speakers forcing everyone to vacate the halls. Five minutes and that small moment of sincere dialogue was over. Granted all that happened was we introduced ourselves, yet I couldn't help but sense that the introduction was deeper than a simplistic "sorry I dropped your books." Perhaps it was the hesitation in his voice when he spoke, or the profound look we gave one another that rendered the sweet smiles that stretched ear to ear. Perhaps I just thought he was cute.

I was cautious not to spend much time thinking of such an insignificant-significant moment, scrolling through apps on my phone to occupy my ever busy mind. Oddly enough Mr. Young had yet to walk in. Which for the time being left me the teacher's assistant to a teacherless class. That time was all too short lived with Mr. Young bombarded in, immediately opening his lesson plans after he called roll.

"Dawson, I don't really have anything for you to do. I'm sorry" Mr. Young said seeming to sincerely think I would somehow be disappointed with that amazing news.

"On no no I understand. It's no problem."

"Are you sure? If you'd like and have anything else you need to do you can go do that, or you can stay here and do whatever. Up to you."

"Thank you. I actually need to take care of something," I responded when truthfully all I needed to take care of was my extreme desire to spend the day in the gym rather than classrooms.

"Alright go ahead. Have a great day" he said like a father saying goodbye to their child.

Seconds later I was on a bee line towards the gym. For some reason I felt the need to dramatize my entrance by kicking the door open. Upon walking in, all that could be heard were the voices of the guys on the basketball court arguing because one of them had apparently missed a pass when he heard me kick in the door. My bad.

The attitude of a grand entrance was now spoiled. Embarrassed, I pulled my phone out of my pocket and pretended to be using it in order to shield myself from the glaring eyes while I walked along the baseline of the court to the bleachers. I sat there, a turtle in its shell, desperately awaiting to be accompanied by anyone. Only the loud discernible words simulating in-game chatter was enough of a motivator for me to take my eyes off of my phone and search for the source. Across the gym a group of girls whom I assumed were freshmen, were practicing for their game later in the day. I had absolutely no clue who they were and quite frankly it didn't matter. They had a volleyball. I started to jump down the stairs cautiously, incidentally creating a very poor rhythm with the sound of my footsteps that resembled an off beat version of the Pink Panther theme song.

With my attention aimed across the building I was met at the bottom of the bleachers with a hand gripping the side of my shoulder, spinning me around.

"Come to my office. I've got some news for you."

I stepped into the office and took a seat in front of the desk. The walls of my torso slowly enclosed around my lungs turning my airway into a straw. Strangely I was panicking, fearing the worst news to come. Even though I knew I that it couldn't be something negative. Right? My fearfulness made breathing a struggle, and talking seemed utterly impossible as it sealed my lips shut. In an attempt to avoid coming off as rude, I found a way to acknowledge her and say, "Hey coach."

"How are you? Ok before I even go any further, do you still want to go to Clemson?" Coach Roberts questioned.

"Yes!" I exclaimed in a tone hinting for her to continue.

"Well I talked to Coach on the phone last night and your name came up. She's really heard a lot about you. I want you to know she said that one of the assistants would be coming to see you play sometime soon."

A loss for words, tingling fingers and a cheeky grin that I unsuccessfully tried to contain revealed the level of exuberance that was feeling. No other words could I muster up other than "I'll be ready."

"That's what I wanted to hear."

Unsure if the conversation was even over, I saw myself out and went to think alone at the top of the bleachers once more. The news had constructed a confidence, a vivacious attitude that instantly grew on me. With the degree of pressure I knew I was going to unintentionally put on myself, I was going to need every last bit of it. This was my goal staring me in the face.

You see my family recently moved to Bluffton about five years ago. All of that time spent here and it took about two weeks to realize that the entire state bleeds either orange or garnet. Maybe it was all of the wonderful yellow sun on the beach that slowly mended my bright red blood into orange. Whatever the case was, almost everything I owned was Clemson. Which my friends back in Alabama had deemed as nothing short of pure betrayal of the Crimson Tide. It was my senior year of volleyball and I'm not sure anything in this world would make me happier than to sign with them. I repeatedly searched for messages or emails from the coaches at Clemson. Every search always came up short. But now it's here. Not sure when nor where, but it's here.

The rest of the day I was hindered to that single thought. Conversation between friends and teachers was reduced to me fabricating any comprehension of whatever subject we were on. Tunnel vision forced me to elude any and all other things that school brought along. At last, I was able to merge myself within the students chaotically exiting the confines of the classrooms at the tone of the last bell.

The time of day slowly gave way to the night. After hours of non-stop worry, my nerves constantly sent me to the bathroom. Shameful and needless to say that didn't suit me very well. End result of that disaster... I was still nervous! Nevertheless, nothing was going to overtake the ongoing nostalgia from earlier. What felt like only moments later, I found myself in the middle of pregame warm-ups. I was going through the motions of it all until I came to the conclusion that it was time to block out anything that wasn't about the task at hand, winning. Just as soon as convinced myself to flip that mental switch I scanned the crowd. The second we made eye contact the stage got bigger.

To my surprise, we were now laying host to Coach Franklin herself. Looking off into the distance and handling a phone call, her presence was instantly impactful. The adrenaline started to overwhelm me, leading me to catch myself looking over at Coach Franklin every other second to see if she was watching. The scoreboard counted down two minutes until game time. The clock was silent yet I mentally heard the ticking of each slow passing second. Somehow two minutes felt like hours. The magnitude that I had set for this moment only magnified the pressure while I briefly meditated. I alone stared at the looking glass of my intellect to calm down and comfort myself. Reflecting on how bad I yearned for this moment, deserved it. Soon the resounding horn drowned out all of my thoughts. I take my spot as the libero, my odd-coloured jersey embraced as my spotlight.

It was another "ball does not touch the floor" kind of night. Laying out for everything I needed to, my body was physically beat up. Dig after dig after dig the pure adrenaline of competition and the magnitude of what could be at stake drive me through the lingering aches that accompanied occasional sharp back pain right above my waist during the seconds between every point that I just chalked up to muscle spasms. My body was in agony but my heart and mind were as happy as could be after the win. At the end of it all, my night was fulfilled with a handshake and a question.

"So Dawson Montgomery, how would you like to be a Clemson Tiger?"

I smiled. Purposefully hesitating to avoid breaking the record for fastest commitment after being offered a scholarship, I looked her in the eyes.

"How soon can I sign?"

Chapter 7: Miranda

Sure I have Brad. I love him with all that I am. But the truth is that I'm more so waiting for him than he is for me. Who am I supposed to go to when I get upset or just want to have that connection with someone? Sure I like to pour all of my feelings out in a letter and send it to Brad, but then what? What good does his "Babe everything will be okay" do for me over a week or two later? Am I wrong for not having the desire to wait a million years while our conversation is delivered through snail mail all because Brad is busy all day, or because he assumed I would think it was a cute idea for us to have some *Dear John* type relationship and write letters as well? You know what they say about the word assume. Plus, I'm not sure he realized that they ended up splitting in the movie. Granted, he's not much of a writer so we text a lot and sometimes I attempt to vent through that, but it feels as though his words have lost a bit of their solace.

I don't know. It could be that I haven't yet grasped the "love knows no time or distance" expression. I just see that in the same way you view being dumped by the love of your life. Then them turning back for only a second to both brutally torture and console your broken heart with "I'll always love you" as they continue to walk further away. It sounds nice. Yet it is simply a gift wrapped way of saying "I'm not going to be here anymore." Now here I am. Far too many miles apart, without as little as a single physical touch to comfort my saudade, I hold my heart in my hand and march through the sunrise and sunset, in a relationship of one.

I've slowly grown accustomed to the let down that that part of my life brings along. The roller coaster of emotions is exhausting, but bearable. After all it's only such a small section of my day I guess. Things could be a lot worse. Like having to wake up and go to fucking high school. That's one of the joys of being smart and early admitting to college. The beautifully horrendous first weeks of the first semester of the year is a pain in the ass. It's the time of the year I like to refer to as *The Times of Two People* . It is a time when the leaves start to refashion themselves into the colors of Fall. On one end you have the moment where disgruntled teens are forced to say goodbye to their summers that were full of long hot days and even longer drunken nights to return to the hell hole that is high school.

The place that is supposedly responsible for the best four years of your life, yet is also known as the place where self esteem, innocence, and dreams go to die. Stupid right? Then on the other hand, you have people like me who have the joy of starting our freshman year of college. We're the ones who have miraculously escaped the captivity of adolescence to venture out on our own. I'm a part of the group who gets to leave home and find themselves in the world.

Its the beginning of the few occasions I will get in life where I have permission to make as many mistakes as possible. I can be reckless and walk around intoxicated or high on a daily basis. For the next four years, this riotous stretch of time allows me to do WHATEVER I want and choose who I want to be in life.

Unfortunately, when you think of college, most people's thoughts were exactly what mine were. The thought that escapes your mind is that it's honestly probably the greatest annoyance and stress of my day. A complicated love life? That I can deal with. But there is no way I can handle one more second of Mr. Green's Intro to Psych course. Don't get me wrong, the first twenty minutes of the year were amazing and pretty interesting. That all went to shit around minute thirty-two. It can't seriously be possible to listen to that monotone base in his voice. Although I must say I actually enjoy the Joker-esque, disturbingly sadistic pitch it changes to whenever he gets excited or tries to add emphasis to phrases. He just talks so much. We have to read so much. As soon as I walk into class, I'm already over it. What happened to "First day of school you'll just go over the syllabus and then go home? Second day you'll still barely do anything. Its super doubtful you'll have homework at all the first week." Mr. Green obviously didn't get the memo.

It's only Wednesday, the second day of this course. After an hour long lecture accompanied by twenty terms, and another twenty-five pages to read and write about as homework, my dislike had heavily set in. It's moments like this where I would love to just sit down and write a letter or have a phone call with Sigmund and Anna Freud, Wilhelm Wundt, William James, Erik

Erikson, and about a dozen other people. I'd just like to express my love for psychology and to thank them for being the reason I'm three days into the school year and am already overloaded with assignments I neither fully understand nor will likely complete on time. You know what? Maybe one of them could tell me why my brain is ready to implode and now I just want to walk up to my room, grab my favorite body pillow and curl into a ball and never have to listen to another thing about the human brain ever again. Its moments where I'm stressed out to this point that there is a legitimate debate that goes on in my head about how day by day the thoughts of becoming a stripper and foregoing college grows just a bit more appealing. Don't judge. We've all thought about it.

Today was seemingly no different. Being one of two technically high school kids in every one of my classes isn't as luxurious as I'd hoped, and a lot more stressful than I'd anticipated. Perhaps I had a bigger problem with that than I did with Freud. Maybe it was safe to say that I did it to myself. I mean after all I chose to spend my senior year in college classrooms over taking a seat beside my friends in high school. "It's better for you to get a jumpstart on college," my parents notioned.

After finishing just the third day of school I can already sense the dissatisfying foretelling of a lackluster routine for days to come. Somehow I just can't seem to help but think that none of it would even matter if I had more motivation to come to at the end of the day. Right now the only motivation I had was that I was one day closer to the weekend. Unfortunately for me, my weekend was currently shaping out to be an abundance of studying, sleep, and binge watching Netflix series; only to leave the solitary confinement of my room to use the bathroom and get food.

My imagination painted the image of myself laying underneath my bed sheets with the fan on full blast. Then after forty-eight hours, I would have nothing to show for my time in that room other than a poor retention of psychology facts; yet I would likely be able to give you a full synopsis of every episode of Scandal. As much as I love Scandal, I grimaced at the thought of how unappealing that weekend sounded. Pondering on things that I could possibly do, my phone vibrated almost perfectly on time. I looked at my screen to see a call from my little sister Lilli.

Nothing short of amusement and curiosity immediately comes when seeing that name. Its fairly safe to say that almost everyone generally has a sibling, a friend, or best friend, but none of them have a Lilli. Someone once said that "No one looks back on their life and remembers the nights they got plenty of sleep." No one has lived these youthful years of their life with this mindset more than she has. There's only a few people who will actually admit that they look up to their younger sibling, but I have no problem stating that. Somehow she managed to have the gregarious, cordial personality that I aimed to be. Unfortunately I seemed to have only managed to be an introvert who has just enough friends to disguise her social awkwardness. I realized our personalities had shaped our social statuses in different ways when some people around town started to refer to me as "Lilli's big sister."

"Hello" I said after finally picking up the phone.

"Yo can I borrow an outfit for the party?" she said.

"You going to that?"

"Yes I think we're all going. I talked to Wyatt and he and James are going. So let's go. Oh what about the shirt you got last weekend?"

Initially my first thought in response was to say no because it was destined that I would be left all alone while her boyfriend Wyatt proceeded to take away the attention from my pitiful lonely self. Then I thought of that probable first awkward moment left alone with James. You know the one where you both look at each other with nothing to say because you both immediately realize that you two are only associated because your best friends are dating one another; so now you're basically friends by default. That moment would one hundred percent happen. Regardless of knowing that future was in store, I neglected to say anything on the account that I also thought I was pretty melodramatic. As I tended to be.

"Alright yea I don't care. I've gotta find something to wear for it too then. We'll figure it out on Friday before we go."

"Ok thanks! I'll talk to you later then. I'll be home later on. I'm out with Wyatt. Love you!"

"Oh ok. Tell him I said hi. Love you too!"

"He said hey."

"Alright. I'll see you later. Love you."

"Ok. Bye. Love you too."

It always seemed to be just that simple. She had this reoccurring thing of helping me figure out my plans since I for some reason seemed incapable of doing it alone. Most of the time those plans resulted in one of us saying "If we get caught, this is what we're going to say." A few sentences and my entire forty-eight hour weekend vacancy was filled. Though the party was on Friday night, that gave me all of Saturday to deal with the hangover I was oddly looking forward to. Then I would be left to confront whatever video, gossip, or ridiculous thing I said from the other night. Which means on Sunday I might want to take a look at that now less important homework. Problem solved.

The days pass and the hours tick by as the sun starts to set on Friday night. I sit on the floor looking into the mirror while putting my makeup on with my playlist blaring from the speaker sitting on my bed. I begin curling my hair when the sound of the front door bursting open stopped my heart and left me motionless. Slowly I put my curling iron down and turned my head towards my bedroom door. Curiosity told me to go see what it was. Fear told me not to be the dumbass from horror movies who thinks it's a good idea to go look. Guess I'm the dumbass.

The eery sound of footsteps began to loom throughout the house. I realized the sound was coming from the living room as the footsteps caused the wood floor to screech. The echo of the steps grew louder as they closed the distance to the staircase. Tip toeing my way down the staircase, I peep my head over the railing to try to get a glimpse into the room, cautious not to be seen. Finally, I decided to just walk down and face whatever awaited. Before my foot ever touched down on the next step, I heard "Tell him I'll beat his ass!" Recognizing the voice immediately, the tension fled my body. Around the corner comes Lilli with her phone in one hand and a two shopping bags in the other.

"Who's that?" I asked.

"James just talking shit in the background."

"Oh. What's in the bag?"

Out of one of the bagsz came a twelve pack of beer. Then she looked at me and grinned, reaching down into the other bag.

"Flamingo beer bong" she laughed while hoisting it up.

My eyes lit up as I glared at it, nodding my head. "Well shit! Soooo, Uber home kind of night?"

Chapter 8: Maddux

With absolutely no knowledge on how to actually host a party, I reverted to the endless party movies I had seen over the years to give me some guidance. Although, I quickly forgot the point of me watching them about fifteen minutes into each, I realized there was only really one universal rule. Get alcohol and a lot of it. Thank God for the money from my summer job and fake I.D., because after a ton of fruit and juice for a full tub of jungle juice, six bottles of vodka, two bottles of whiskey, a bottle of rum, a keg, and my own personal bottle of Grey Goose to sip on for the night, the charge on my debit card wouldn't have been a pretty subject for a family meeting. Not to mention that to the clerks at the liquor store I definitely look like a raging alcoholic now.

8:30 p.m. rolls around while I continue to set up the bottles in the kitchen. Due to it being the only alcohol I cared about for the night, I placed the Grey Goose in the mini fridge that was in my room. I proceeded to make my way back to take out all of the fruit and slice them into small pieces; one by one tossing them into the clear plastic tub I bought earlier. After countless oranges, strawberries, pineapples, kiwi, and a number of fruit juices and cheap vodka, the tub was almost completely filled. Soon after the entire room smelled of a weird, yet satisfying aroma of citrus, berries, and vodka. A LOT of vodka. I grabbed a cup from the pantry and dipped it into tub to fill my glass. The scent grew stronger as I pulled the cup closer to have a taste. My body shivered after the sip, almost as if to wake my body up in preparation of the night to come. After one small sip, it quickly turned into a complete refill of the cup. The taste of fruit seemed to overwhelm the alcohol and I wondered if I should add more. Though six liters of vodka seemed to be enough. Right?

Quickly my attention turned to my phone. By the seconds my phone was blowing up with messages from people asking "When do you want people to come?" or "Are a lot of people coming?" One after another I replied to numerous people answering the same questions repetitively. After a while I got sick of it and just decided to tell people to start coming around 10:00p.m. Unfortunately I didn't think that out very well being that it was only ten minutes away and I still had to clear out the vases as well as literally anything of value and move it into the closet of my parent's room. I began rushing in and out of rooms, grabbing as many items as my hands could hold, being lucky to somehow not drop anything in transit. Finally 10:05 p.m. comes and I grab another cup of jungle juice to reward myself.

The reward however, was short lived when I started hearing sounds outside from music and cars entering the driveway. There was a knock at the door. Once mysterious murmurs grew into identifiable voices that stand await on the other side the closet I got. I opened the door to the sight of about fifty people - beer in hand - ready to get fucked up. My ridiculous initial thought was to question whether they had all planned to show up at the same time. The next thought? "So it begins!"

"Come in" I said while holding the door open for them to walk inside. "Just put your beer anywhere in the kitchen. Cups are on the table. Pool is out back." Just as I finished my words, another wave of vehicles pulled up. With no intention on holding the door open for everyone who would come in, I walked back inside and let the door shut behind me. "They'll just walk in" I thought, hoping to be right. Right I was.

Soon after I found myself sitting around the table with a ton of people playing Give or Take. I turn over a card from the take side. Nine of spades. Looking down at the nine of diamonds, I grimaced knowing that was my signal for nine drinks. Everyone was playing with beer while I made the ever so smart decision to drink my Grey Goose directly out of bottle. It was fun. A pretty hard buzz after a couple rounds yet nothing terrible. But nine long sips of vodka can start to do a number on the body quickly. I stand up from my chair, staggering a bit, and take an overview of the house just to make sure everything was still going well. While my living room played host to the line of leg stands, I watched numerous people funneling beer, a few taking jello shots in the kitchen, there were even a couple of girls by the sink drinking beer out of a flamingo. Immediately, I marked that up on my to do list. I turn my head towards the hallway and see some guy barreling through the bodies in their way. Eventually he made his way through the crowd and now in plain sight. I take a look back down at the cards and reach to flip another over. Just as my hand touched the card I look up to see the guy standing over me and everyone staring at the two of us with their phones out.

"Do you need something?" I asked.

Without answering question he grabs my bottle of Goose and starts to chug as everyone counts the seconds. Initially, all I cared about was the fact that this guy was chugging my alcohol that I just spent thirty-five dollars on. Like what the fuck!

" Eleven! Twelve! Thirteen! Fourteen! Fifteen!" they scream as he finally puts the bottle down. I knew that I only had about twenty seconds to figure out what was even happening and then do something about. I quickly recalled everything in my mind while trying to drown out the cheers of everyone in the house.

"Random guy comes up, drinks my vodka while people count and cheer, then stares me down as of there was only one viable response to what just happened. Did I just get called out in front of everyone at my own party?" I thought. I looked around to see eyes glaring at me from each corner of the room. "I think so" I said to myself. "If you don't do anything then you'll just be the guy got bitched at his own party. Thats going to stick with you. Is that what you want?"

I grabbed the bottle, laughed and took a deep breath.

"One! Two! Three! Four!" they shouted. While they counted closer to fifteen I made the decision that I couldn't just drink to sixteen. I had to drink to something that I hoped no one else was ever willing to drink to. That way I NEVER have to do this again.

"Thirty-three! Thirty-four! Thirty-Five!"

Completely engulfed in the moment, I jumped from my seat and slammed the now empty bottle on to the table and darted towards the door, hi-fiving everyone I passed. Then I zoned out.

I have absolutely no idea how much time had passed or what took place, but when I came back to reality I was a mile down the road, shirtless, with my headphones in, jogging in place in the YMCA parking lot. Instantly regretting my apparent desire to do cardio for no exact reason, I jogged back to the house. The countless animal noises that came from the woods only feet away from sidewalk began to freak me out to the degree that I started jogging in the middle of the road until I finally made it home. Upon arriving back, I found my shirt in the middle of the driveway. I opened the door, cringing in preparation to find a completely trashed house. To my luck everything was exactly how I left it. Well, at least how I think I remember leaving it. I found a seat on the couch and immediately all of the adrenaline and hype vanished. All I was left with was the feeling of a half bottle of Goose fermenting in my stomach. I battled to hold my head up as it swayed uncontrollably.

Struggling to breathe normally because of my stomach twisting in knots and the nausea only getting worse, I found myself literally crawling on the floor to the bathroom down the hall. After having my hands and feet stepped on by seemingly everyone in my path, I sat on the floor of the bathroom with my head in toilet desperately trying to gag myself for any kind of relief. Sadly, all I managed to do was spit in the toilet a few times and accomplish nothing. I leaned my back up against the bathtub and looked towards the ceiling, hopeless, regretful, and in pure agony from the torture my body was in. The entire room turned into a roundabout going a hundred miles per hour. For a second, I thought I was moving sporadically, until I called down and recognized that I hadn't moved an inch. I sat in misery for the next few minutes until deciding to give it one last try at vomiting next morning's hangover away. Once again, I just found myself spitting until the bathroom door opened.

"Oh shit are you alright?" she said.

"Ehh I'm not feeling so well" I mustered out.

"Well, do you mind if I go pee?"

"Yea I don't care. Umm what's your name?" I said in the most slurred manner.

"Miranda?" she replied.

"Okay. Umm Miranda, can you tell these people to leave? I'm too fucked up to try and shout."

"Umm sure. But can you move so I can pee?"

"Can't move. Have... to throw up." I said while throwing my body back to lean up again.

"You aren't even throwing up? You're just spitting in the toilet."

"You can pee, but I'm not moving. I'm sorry I can't."

"I don't really know you other than I know this is your party. So I'm not just going to pee beside you. Thats...that's kind of weird. That's actually really weird. Can you just move?"

"Can't." I murmured while slowly dozing off. I opened my eyes for a second to look her in the face. "You're cute though." Then my head tilted back and I fell into unconsciousness. Goodnight.

Chapter 9

"Are you ok?" Miranda asked while quickly stepping towards him to check.

"Hey. Are you alright?" she questioned again, shaking his body gently. No response came from Maddux. The only indication of life were his occasional groans and faint breathing that resembled breathing through a straw. Her once gentle shrugs soon turned into shoves that rattled his insensate body back and forth. She began to slap his face, leaving her handprint on the side of his pale face, but to no avail. Miranda continued to rock him until her movements finally caused the back of his head to thump against the tub just hard enough to get him to creep open his eyes.

Maddux struggled to keep his eyes open as he sat. His cognition blurred and completely washed of any thoughts outside of the aching pain of his body. After glaring at Maddux with his head tilted over the side of the bathtub, and being mildly cautious and neglectful to leave him for the worry of him slipping into a sleep, Miranda caressed her hand on his face, moving her hand to shake his head slowly in order to be more calm in her effort to make sure he was still alright.

"I'm about to go get some help. Just wait here."

She walked back into the living room, questioning why she had just told a near unconscious person to wait where they were. Where was he going to go? Through the crowd of bodies which made up the party that now had effortlessly grown to somewhere over two hundred people, Miranda spotted James, Wyatt, and Lilli in the distance occupying the couch in the corner of the living room next to the coffee table. From the scene, it looked as though James was in a similar state as Maddux. James sat hunched over the arm of the couch, asleep, having to use his arm to prop himself up with his head in his hand, with his mouth slightly opened while he breathed heavily through it, each breath seemingly deeper than the last and his snoring being heard faintly within the noise of the party.

"What's wrong with him?"

"What do you mean? Dude just chugged vodka with that kid. Now he's like this," Wyatt said sarcastically.

"Well we've got a situation. I mean it's not really our problem but I'd feel bad if we just leave him in there like that. So Maddux is on the bathroom floor and he might be even worse than James. I don't want to just leave him because I'm honestly kind of scared something may happen to him if he's just left there."

"Sooo what exactly are you wanting to do?" Lilli replied.

"I don't know. I mean he's already home so I guess we can just help him to his room or something then wait a bit and make sure nothing happens." Miranda said, seemingly unsure of her idea. "But he asked me to get everyone out of the house."

She whistled, echoing throughout the house. The music stopped and the hundred people filling the center of the house changed their eyes to focus on her, with heads even being turned towards the inside of the house by the mass of people at the pool right outside of the screen door that sectioned off from the living room.

"Maddux said everyone needs to leave!"

A silence filled the room while everyone looked at each other, confused on what they should do which encompassed small chatter amongst the crowd. Each person seemed to look around the house, waiting for any sort of indication of people beginning to leave. All this resulted in was a house full of teenagers standing in place and no one being willing to be the first to walk out.

"Yo shotgun these with me!" someone yelled. Miranda's words went void as the music turned back on and the party commenced. The entire party scene erupted once more. In the matter of seconds,the vibrations from the speakers could be felt underneath their feet, eight people had managed to call downs on the beer pong table, decks of cards were out as new game of Ring of Fire started, and teams were starting to form for Flip Cup.

Frustrated she walked down the hall and stepped into the bathroom, causing her to be out of sight. She waited a moment, then ran back into the living room and screamed "Everyone shut the fuck up! Maddux just said the cops are on their way here! Get the hell out!"

Recognizing the seriousness in her tone, people filed their way out of the house. Everywhere you looked, teens rushed to grab what was left of the alcohol they brought, as well as grabbing some of what others had left. A couple of them felt the need to do one last leg stand to cap off a great night, while others leaped out of the pool, bringing puddles of water along with them as they sprinted through the house. One by one each of them found their way to exit the premises until eventually the house was vacant, trashed, and in desperate need of wet floor signs.

"Get your stuff let's go." Lilli said.

"Help me get James to the car. Come on." Wyatt added.

"What are you all rushing me for?" Miranda noted.

"You saying you just want to be standing here when the police show up?" Wyatt asked.

"What? No I was lying to get everyone to leave. There's no cops coming. Honestly I thought I told you that was my plan. Maybe that was just in my head. Sorry. You can sit James back down now."

Wyatt and Lilli stared at Miranda with a look of disbelief, letting go of James as he slithered down from their arms like a shoulder bag back on to the spot of the couch where he then sprawled out to rest. Miranda led the group through the house to search for Maddux. She cracked open the bathroom door, only to find it to be empty.

"He's not in here" she said as she turned towards Wyatt and Lilli.

"Maybe he went to his room?" Lilli replied.

"Well I'm going to go look for him just in case. It would be funny but hopefully he didn't take off running with all the people that were leaving," Miranda laughed.

The thoughts of possibly finding him in a worse state than when she left him began to surface in her head. Marching through the hallway, she flung open every door, each time yelling "Maddux!" in dyer hope for some echoing response. Midway down the hall was a staircase that wound up to the second floor of the house. Drunk in her own right, and always finding amusement from simple things, she methodically attempted to step only on every other step, exaggerating the distance between steps by extending her back leg while she lunged forward to the next, letting her arms reach ahead of her as some sort of way to propel her forward while all they truly did was flail in the air. When she neared the top on the stairs, she saw what looked like a single all white Nike Air Force One shoe right outside of an open door with the lights on. Finally approaching the door, Miranda recognized the other shoe placed underneath the thick glass coffee table angled toward heaps of clothing that sprawled throughout the floor to another bathroom. Shirts dangled from the edge of the sink. Piles of socks laid stuffed within the spacing between the door and tile floor. Shorts, pants, underwear, while hoodies and sweatshirts concealed the rest of the floor. At the center of the bathroom, directly in front of the toilet, a plastic white clothes basket was pushed over -with clothes seeping out of it - on to the stack of shorts and right beside it laid Miranda's newfound drunken friend, Maddux. Somehow amidst all of the chaos, Maddux had managed to make his way upstairs. Only to now find himself passed out on the floor of clothes, in fetal position, with his head slightly resting inside of the basket, and strangely enough, completely naked.

Birthday suit, in the bluff, skinny-dip ready, we're going streaking in the quad, NAKED.

It was extremely probable that another Snapchat moment such as this - one so infamous, hilarious, and memorable - would never show its face and present itself like this again. "Am I a bad person?" Miranda debated with herself. Meanwhile, she whipped out her phone, turning it at different angles trying to manipulate the bathroom lighting for the best quality.

"Somebody drank a little too much" she laughed as she stepped over the mountain of clothes, zooming in and out onto Maddux.

It only took a few seconds before Wyatt and Lilli were storming upstairs to the scene. Simultaneously, Maddux rose from his bed of laundry.

"Why.. in the fuck.. is he naked?" Lillie screamed while simultaneously shielding her eyes from seeing any more of him than she already had.

"You're the kid who drank the rest of that Grey Goose with James! Right?" Wyatt laughed while snapchatting the scene.

Maddux, quickly grabbing sweatpants from the floor to cover up, with his nervousness and embarrassment showing in his complexion, stuttered saying "I don't really know why I'm naked to be honest. The last thing I remember was someone yelling that there were cops on the way and I somehow sobered up for ten seconds to run to my room and uhh yea, that's me. Not very smart and never again."

"Nah not at all but it was nice as hell though. I'll never do it but it was fun watching y'all. But my bad man I'm drawing a blank. What's your name?"

"Maddux."

"I'm Wyatt. This is my girl Lilli." He said gesturing to his side to Lilli. "Then the dude you were drinking with is our boy James. I may forget your name, but I'll remember you for the Grey Goose for sure. Goose. I like that. That's what I'm gonna call you from now on. That cool?"

"Goose? Yea I like it too. I can get use to that."

Miranda motioned to Wyatt and Lilli, pointing down the stairs.

"Well Goose as much of a pleasure as it is to sit here and chat with you half naked, our friend is currently down stairs and we should probably go down there to make sure he hasn't died. But thank you for having us. It was great!"

"No problem! Sorry about all this but thank you for checking on me tonight. Means a lot."

"Always. I'm sure I'll see you soon."

They walked downstairs only to find James still completely unconscious with his body folded like a lawn chair. His face smashed against the floor yet somehow his lower half still managed to be on the couch.

Wyatt grabbed him and put James's arm around him to drag him to the car.

"Lets go bud."

Chapter 10: Miranda

It has become so commonplace in my family that I can't make myself believe that only I, and not everyone has had a million moments where the subject of college arises and some member of their family talks about themselves and how during their college years they could drink whiskey by the handle to the point that their roommates started thinking Jack Daniels was the name of their best friend or boyfriend from back home, and vodka cranberries were consumed at the pace of an elementary student with an access to endless Capri Suns. Sleep was as foreign to them as the old Cartoon Network and Nickelodeon is to a kid born in the 2000s. Studying consisted of sitting in their dorm room, locked away from the world, cigarette or blunt by the ash tray that lay in the window, with all of the songs performed by Queen on shuffle. Always, always starting with *Bohemian Rhapsody* and strategically skipping to *Under Pressure* when they got to a subject they couldn't understand in order to both lighten the mood of cramming for an exam and a way for them to lip sync and dance themselves into a much needed break.

Then, they give you the harsh life lesson and reality of how one day in their mid-twenties to early thirties all of that completely vanished and they found themselves struggling to move out of bed while dealing with the constant aching of their body. Their heads became one with the toilet as they puked the previous night away. Then they unfortunately ruin good stories when they try to quote things constantly heard by teens in order to seem as though they are still "with the times" by saying something like "I always said I was here for a good time, not a long time." I mean thank you for the life lessons Uncle Jerry and Aunt Jan but no, you didn't always say that. Because Drake - Champagne Papi himself - said it first! Plus I'm pretty sure he was that elementary kid with endless Capri Suns you spoke of from your college years.

Regardless, I'm hoping they just exaggerated the ages in which it finally hit them that they couldn't do it like they used to. I just started but I guess that eighteen years old nowadays feels a lot like thirty because my head is throbbing and I'm currently only staying alive with the help of my hangover survival kit of Pedialyte and alka-seltzer plus. The party was Friday. Seriously, are three day hangovers even a thing? I mean yea I drank a bit on Saturday, and of course mimosas on Sunday because you know, I like to do classy shit like that. Even though I'm pretty sure mimosas are more so just for the morning and not a substitute for every drink of my Sunday Funday. So maybe three days in a row wasn't the greatest idea, but it damn sure was a great time.

With my head stuffed into my pillow I reached my hand over the edge of my bed and repeatedly push my finger on buttons on my alarm clock sitting on my nightstand until it was finally quiet an gave me some some quick headache relief. I rushed to the bathroom to beat Lilli, knowing I had only seconds before she claimed the entire bathroom as hers to get ready; leaving me to wait on the other side banging on the door until mom yelled for me to stop. I got six feet from the door and then a pair of socks spread across the hardwood floors turned me into an uncoordinated individual who looked as if it were their first time in the ice. My arms flailing around ridiculously in my awful attempts to gather my balance until I stunned my toes on the bathroom door which led to a painful fall which only grew more painful as I could hear Lilli's laughter as she jumped over my body to open the door and take over the bathroom.

"Hope you're ok. You suck!" she joked.

Suddenly it occurred to me that I had only hit the snooze button as I could hear the never-ending beeping of my alarm. As I lay there on the floor I faced the fact that I was not at all ready for today. So now as per my physically lazy wish and my final piece of hangover advice to myself, I've decided to use my mulligan on dressing up for school if the powers that be will so graciously allow it. Hope my classmates like messy buns, oversized Salty Dog sweatshirts and ninja turtle pajamas.

It didn't even take me two seconds upon being fully entered into my first class room to hear what sounded like a terrible burlesque of someone who could actually sing. I look around the corner to see this short girl dancing in the room. With her eyes closed and her rose gold headphones latched to her ears, she swung her hips to the music. Her predisposed joyous personality was infectious as her wavy auburn hair swayed uncontrollably. She turned around and the color in her face washed out, leaving a traumatized look of embarrassment on her lightly freckled pale face. Her calm hazel eyes filled with shame. Slowly creeping back out of the shy shell she had suddenly buried into, she mustered up her words.

"Hey I'm really sorry. I promise I'm not usually this awkward. I'm Dawson by the way. I sit ... back there," she said while pointing to the desk in the back of the room near the window that overlooked the entrance of the building.

"I'm Miranda, and oh thats a shame. I was really looking forward to having someone around to join in all my weirdness," I replied.

"Oh my God I am so happy to hear that. Because honestly I lied. I'm normally this awkward," she laughs. "I'm probably the weirdest person I know."

In the time that ensued we spoke of how we shared the thought that the real tragedy of the movie Titanic was how selfish Rose was and that there were about twenty ways for them both to fit.

"She's still more likable than the biggest pussy in literary or cinematic history in Edmund Pevensie." Dawson laughed.

With those words she sparked my ever long rant of how angry I get every time I choose to watch that movie; how I shout at every single thing Edmund does until I end up calling my sister into the room just saw I can pause it. I know it's just a movie, and that means I probably have a huge problem, but for anyone who's seen the movie or read the book, you completely understand my endless frustration. And Dawson did.

She stared at me, almost as if she were listening to something peculiar or had just seen a strange animal and replied, "Ok I know the actor who played Edmund was only doing his job, but I still feel like if I were to see him in person, I'm not so sure I would be so nice, even if he was the friendliest man alive. He would be like

'Hey. How are you doing today?' While having a huge smile on his face. Meanwhile I believe the only thing that would process in my brain to say back to him would be 'Shut up! I know what you did to Mr. Tumnus!' Then I'd continue to walk away."

It didn't take much longer for me to realize that Dawson was going to be a special person in my life. Fortunately for me, she became exactly that and more. In an instant, she went from being a blissful stranger to a friend.

Unfortunately for us our newfound friendship didn't cause for class to be cancelled. Time ensued as students began piling into the classroom; each one mumbling about how they were not really ready to present or bragged of how they crammed in the entire project early this morning. After a brief and very underwhelming presentation, I retreated to the back of the room until 9:50 a.m appeared and sprinted from the room like someone who actually had somewhere to be. Dawson followed behind me, her head tilted down while her arms tightly clutched her books.

"It was nice meeting you!" she said in her soft voice with a sincere smile vibrant on her face.

"You too. We should hang out soon!"

"Sounds good!"

Chapter 11: James

If there is anything that sets the vibe of my day, it's the sunrise peaking through my blinds and onto my face, illuminating the rest of my room. It is very much the one thing that can't be unseen. Once it has burned my eyes while I try to wipe away the moat from the corners of my eyelids, it's all over from there. No more five more minutes type situations for me or anything. However, it's definitely not any motivation to get out of bed either but sometimes that glow radiating on my cheeks leads me to get my day going. So I guess it is a motivator, just not the type I typically enjoy.

Although the morning sunrise and I had formed a bit of a frenemies relationship, I looked forward to each and every sunset that came. It was something that my family and I always seemed to do as often as we could. Dad would always stop by and buy ice cream before we went to the beach. We would get there and talk about our day and the events that followed. Most families did that same thing at the dinner table, but we preferred to be a little different. We would laugh and joke, and the days when it was still warm we would run into the water. It was during these moments I learned to fall in love with sunsets. As we looked on, my dad would always remind me to let go of all of the negative things from the day, whether they be thoughts, feelings, or actions and let them fade away with the sunset.

We started that routine when I was about five years old and now it's twelve years later and here I am driving to Coligny Beach around five o'clock to sit on a towel and pretend to do homework. While in reality I was only there for a perfect view of the sunset. I arrived on the beach to luckily see that it wasn't crowded so isolating myself wouldn't be too hard. I put the towel down and grabbed my tablet from my bag and sat it to my side. I scrolled through the playlist in my phone until I finally decided and then I continued on to be mesmerized by the plum and orchid colors of the sky. Ironically the same place that my dad had brought me to to teach me how to forget thoughts, had now become the place I came to think.

This day didn't provide any dissimilar thoughts than any of the previous. I had gone to school, tried my best to be attentive and active before finally zoning out into that world where only the most melancholy of thoughts reside. Then to try to counteract fall into that trans, I would speak to other classmates. It would work up until the embarrassing moment of my teachers calling my name asking the ridiculous question "Do you want to fill the rest of the class in on what you're talking about?" The sarcasm in that question only inspired sarcastic answers like "No I don't want to. That's exactly why I'm only talking to Emily, Tristan, and Cody." Which is the answer I would give if I knew my mom wouldn't break my neck with the slap she would give me the second she saw me again. Instead I kept the thought in mind and the sadness that occupied it was now accompanied by frustration. Either choice I made was and would never be the right choice. So throughout all of that, I was right back here in the beach playing my sad songs with a clouded mind and heavy heart.

I stared off into the sunset with the wind creating a feeling over my shoulders reminiscent of my father pulling me in for a hug. I went on to ask myself the same question I always do when sitting here. What is it about these thoughts, these feelings, this pain that you are almost choosing not to let go? Maybe because when I was learning to let go, they were always things that I had the ability to make better or reconcile the next day. If I wasn't able to do any of those things, it was probably a situation I would rather leave left in the past because I didn't care about it. But this I cared about. Out of the million moments that had come and gone with my dad that I had the chance to reconcile, finally the moment came where I messed up and then no longer had that opportunity. It would be such a simple fix if I had the chance. However I will never see the day that presents me that chance. Then almost insanely I answered that response again and go on to begin this two person conversation with only myself. Momentarily I came to conclusions that I assumed would be the answers to all of my problems. You know, since sad music and isolation wasn't doing the trick. On this episode of my thoughts on the beach I realized that while being alone my mind crumbled me. Then I remembered Dawson's FCA speech about a week ago. She reiterated the fact that we aren't alone. I knew she meant a feeling and if I could be isolated and not feel as such, I would do it in a heartbeat. So church events was now on the table to try to help.

The clocked ticked by and the sun lowered disappeared behind the ocean curtain. In my mind, my idea it was pretty outlandish and far fetched, but there was no downfall. If it doesn't work, now

I get to spend time and see Dawson. If it works, it was killing two birds with one stone.

Time passed and another Tuesday night gave way to the light of a Wednesday morning sunrise. I rushed to the school to get a decent seat in the auditorium. This time, it was Pastor Montgomery who took the stage as I could spot Dawson nearby in the front row. I honed into every word that came out of his mouth. Even finding myself taking notes on my phone to look up later. Which now that I think of it, probably looked disrespectful to some of they didn't know what I was doing. The meeting concluded and as students stood up to file out of the building Pastor Montgomery asked if anyone would like to join FCA. I knew this wasn't my normal kind of thing and truthfully I wasn't sure whether they would make me get up and talk but I also noticed that I had gone two separate services and not the first thought spiral, or distraction in sight. I walked down the isle where Dawson stood holding the clipboard. I was met halfway.

Pastor Montgomery looked at me and extended his hand.

"How are you doing today? I'm Pastor Montgomery."

His grip was extremely firm, almost cracking the bones on the sides of my palm. It was as if he was trying to prove some kind of point. I looked him in the eyes and shook his hand as best I could without indicating the discomfort I was feeling.

"I'm James. I'm doing well. Nice to meet you."

"Are you looking to join us in FCA?"

"Yes sir but to be honest I don't know much or near enough to be able to get up there and talk."

"Oh that's alright. That's what we're here for. I'll introduce you to everyone."

He motioned me down the aisle where a group of ten stood waiting. Dawson front and center.

"This is my daughter Dawson, she's our President. This is Tristan our .."

I cut him off in shock.

"Daughter?"

Chapter 12

Every Tuesday and Thursday, at 2:45 p.m. in classroom 102 of the agricultural building FCA would meet to discuss the bible, future events and who was speaking the following Wednesday. Every time there were numerous people giving their input on subjects that James hadn't been able to even think about including himself in.

How could he possibly be able to jump into conversations about creating a subject based on trust by referencing Peter and Jesus walking out on the water or how you could potentially take the story of Samson and relay it to the student body to give them a message about strength? Instead he sat there, for forty five minutes every single meeting and had to bite his tongue while constantly catching the stares of everyone in the room who knew how out of place he was just as much as he did. So he made a point to learn more, study more, listen instead of spending his time in that room distracted by the uncontrolled actions of the rest of the room. Unfortunately, he wasn't having great luck with that idea.

It wasn't until one day after one of the meetings that Dawson recognized the frustration on his face while flipping through pages of the Bible reading and taking down notes that things began to shift.

She examined him and waited for a moment where his frustration seemed to make him take a pause from the reading and said "You look like you're studying pretty hard there."

With his hands behind his head, a scowl on his face and leaning back as far as the chair would allow he replied, "I am. But I'm done reading because it's like I get to the fifteenth verse and forget what the second verse said. So then I have to write notes. It's just driving me crazy."

"Maybe if you read it like a book that you want to enjoy, rather than a textbook, it will be easier. I don't know anyone who can sit here and quote a textbook. But if you asked them to quote a John Green book then you couldn't get them to shut up. Make it easier for yourself sweetheart."

"Well could you help me along the way on top of that?"

"Of course."

Slowly, a relationship started to bloom. It was from that point, that the two finally gave themselves an excuse to be inseparable. And so it began.

It wasn't long before James was starting to insert himself into the discussions with actual points. He always included himself humbly, forever afraid of saying something far from correct and making a fool of himself. Soon after he was leading the group in prayer, even beginning talks of him possibly speaking soon at a morning service. He was proud of himself. Not only for his progression with FCA but for winning a battle mentally that he felt he had been losing for years.

What used to be an everyday takeover for at least a while was now simmered to every other day or few days. He could go about his day without his thoughts spiraling and bothering him in all of the random ways they normally did. He could watch baseball and not be stuck on the thought of how he wished for his dad to sit alongside his mom in the stands for his senior season. The replay of their last conversation became something that came up to haunt him less each day. However, James had always referred to his thought spirals and ongoing problems as his demons. He viewed them like their own separate entities. That is exactly why even though he felt he was winning this battle, he couldn't help but remain alert.

Somehow the thoughts - though not coming in abruptly and uninvited like normal - had now only surfaced to his head by his own thinking. The longer the thoughts went without becoming a nuisance, they seemed to be at the forefront of James's thinking. Because he awaited the time they came back. He wondered why the temptations of being under the influence seemed so uninteresting. How could it be that he was now rolling out of bed without the lethargic movement and crippled mind to roll back over and throw the sheets over his head, hoping for his dreams to extend into the late hours so he wouldn't have to face the day?

Why couldn't he accept that maybe things were actually going well? Instead he viewed it as a tease. He saw it as a conspiracy that he was being toyed with by being given a freedom to be happy, only for it to be taken from him in an instance. He looked for that negative humbling at every corner. So much so that less became more. The less his mind was taken over as it once did, the more he focused on all of the reasons why they must be right around the corner. No matter what, he never gave himself peace. He questioned whether he saw things clearly, or if he was simply losing his mind with every passing second. There were only moments in his day that he found peace and a genuine happiness. His friends, and Dawson. His friends motivated him to continue while Dawson not only gave ammo to face the world's battles, but provided a fortress to protect him from it as well. More so, he found a love in her, that was unmatched.

James wouldn't consider himself a sapiophile by any means, but there was undeniably a certain mental stimulation that sparked whenever Dawson got into deep conversation on topics that she was passionate about. When she spoke of things in the Bible or even when we spoke about music and she went through her list of under-appreciated artists, created another level to his attraction.

Her knowledge, pure conviction and artistic outlook of things were just as prepossessing as the aesthetic glow in her eyes when the light struck them from the side of her face. Her beauty invited him closer, but her pure soul kept him there.

For both of them, as the days grew longer, their affection grew fonder, while also leaving their hearts and minds completely dazed and confused. How was it that every though that her presence seemed to fight the same negative that haunts them when they are alone?

As for Dawson, the moment they were apart, her pain broke her down. Sometimes the pain wrapped her spine like a blanket. There were the moments that every nerve in her back lit up at once causing the feelings of a thousand needles piercing her skin. The only thing that eased her pain were the steroids she was given for her pain that she realized had slowly started to make her gain weight. The weight started at her stomach and made its way to her thighs until showing in her cheeks; it made a once confident girl whose competitive fire began to waver with her having to sit and watch her team compete while she was forced to sit on the side. While her future coach kept in touch with her and assured her place with Clemson, Dawson still felt uneasy.

However, while the pain and numbness had become a new normal, the pain felt bearable when they were together. The pain even subsided after a while, only coming in bursts. So she yearned for those moments as they became a fuel for positivity. She looked forward to going and teaching James and getting to know him. It was never the big things that drew her to him. She lived for the small moments in time when they would make eye contact when a light bulb when off in his brain and he understood the message in whatever Bible lesson we were on for the day. She started to learn all of his insecurities; which those insecurities grew to be her favorite images of him. Images like the small gap between his front teeth that you could only notice when he had a good laugh or showed off an impressive and gentle smile. She thought about the moments he would cringe as she ran her fingers up and down the side of his hand to feel his skin raised beside his pinky fingers where his extra fingers used to be from being born with polydactyly. Although James himself couldn't stand the thought of it, he seemed to enjoy how amazing she oddly believed it to be. She adored the way it seemed as though there wasn't a song made in history that he didn't know. She fell in love with the daily concerts they had in her car. She even loved his growing frustration when ever she tickled his body, or the fish out of water movements when she tickled his feet. She loved everything.

Two separate struggles. Two separate mental battles. But both of them diminished by a love that was one in the same.

Chapter 13: Dawson

I awaken from my sleep to see the ever annoying Netflix question "Are you still watching?" I move my hand toward the controller to click yes as it turns the scene to Barney being lectured about love by Robin on another episode of How I Met Your Mother. It's 1:20a.m. on a Wednesday morning and I have absolutely no business being up knowing that I present to FCA again in six hours. I rest my head between the pillows, one leg out of the blanket of course and attempt to waste more hours sleeping. To no avail I toss and turn until I forced myself to accept the fact that my day had begun. Throwing my legs on the floor I stood up, only to immediately be sat back down. The room spun as my vision grew hazy as I crashed right back onto the bed.

There I lay in bed. Until momentarily I awake, only to roll over from my side to my stomach. Immediately, my body cringes. "Mom! Dad!" I screamed. That same excruciating pain shot throughout my spine, radiating into my legs and right arm. I was frozen, and literally incapable of moving under my own power.

My parents burst open the door. "What's wrong?!"

Mustering up my words through the pain, tears forming, I slowly said "I woke up and tried to roll over. I can't move. Anything."

They rushed to me. My mom grabbed me by the waist as my dad gently wrapped his arms around my back and shoulders. Slowly they began to turn my body and sit me up. It was as if someone were driving ice picks through different parts of my spine, causing thr rest of my body to shut down.

"Thank you" I said after finally getting situated. "I'm sorry."

"Honey, don't be sorry" mom said while resting her hand on my shoulder.

"Your appointment is at 10 o'clock tomorrow but we're going now. As soon as you feel better we're leaving. We're just going to a hospital, so don't worry about changing."

The next few moments felt like years. Random spasms and sharp pains neglected any brief comfort. Eventually the time came where I had enough.

"Ok let's go. I've gotta go."

They helped me out of bed. Then each put an arm around me, walking me from my room to the car. My legs were weak, and seemed almost useless. They felt the same kind of weak that you have whenever you finally get a cast taken off and you haven't used that body part in a while. I hated it. We drove to the hospital. Even though I'm not sure if I was more scared of the pain I was in, or watching my dad swerve in and out of lanes between cars at 80 miles per hour.

We pulled up to the emergency door. Mom rushed in to notify the nurses and get a wheelchair for me while dad stayed to help me out. After a long delay of questions and going through the entire check in process, the doctors finally ran me back to the Radiology room for an Computerized Tomography scan on my spine. Forty minutes of lying in pain. Forty minutes of the most annoying sound imaginable. Of all days to forget headphones, this most definitely was not the day. I couldn't help but think of endless scenarios of what could be wrong. "

Was it scoliosis? Degenerative spine condition? Cancer? Slipped disk? Broken back? Or was it just that I'm just a huge baby and it's nothing more than a really bad case of back spasms? Then the other worries arised. What about volleyball? Will they still want me? I just committed so can they wouldn't just drop me. Right?"

Once the test was over they brought me back to my room. I sat in there for hours, waiting alongside my parents. Then he came in. He was a large man, but had a smile that made him gentle. He had brown hair a baby face which didn't seem to completely fit his stature. He was a six foot baby face whose image I believed leaned more towards teddy bear rather than grizzly.

"Hi, I'm Dr. Hitchman."

"How are you?"

"Doing well. I took a quick look at the images from your CT scan."

He then sighed and put his head down, seeming to brace even hisself for his next words. His body language alone made my chest tense. A look of conviction lined his face as slowly shook his head while he scanned the papers.

"You have two different masses on your spinal cord. Normally we would schedule surgery to have them removed. But in your case, the tumors are not necessarily big at the moment but rather in slightly difficult areas around the spinal cord that causes for extra precaution. Now, we can monitor it and make sure it is not growing or causing more damage. Because of this our options are different due to the risks that are involved in a surgery like this. Now we haven't done the test yet to determine whether they are benign or malignant, but in this case, due to the fact that the tumors are neurofibroma the chances of it being malignant are low. But as of right now, there is a decision to go in and remove the masses, or because of their size, we can prescribe a corticosteroid to you and we can not have the surgery in hopes that the corticosteroids will limit swelling and and help with pain while hopefully allowing us a better opportunity at successfully removing them later or they could potentially shrink the tumors as well. However, even though you won't have surgery for the time being, it could be a risk. Especially with us not yet knowing the growth rate of the tumors, though they typically are known to grow slowly, with this option you give a little more time to possibly grow and slowly cause damage.

"So either I'm fixed or paralyzed or have some kind of nerve damage? I'm other words I have surgery, you d's obvious to me." I said to cut him off challenge his assessment.

I wasn't even sure why I was acting so tough. My heart sank through the floor. My chest entrapped itself, closing in around my lungs. I thought of so many things, but never this.

"Well we shouldn't speculate anything like that. We just have to weigh out our options and decide on what's best for you." Dr. Hitchman replied. "At the moment, I believe that we should do our best to remove as much of the tumors as possible. Then try radiation therapy but get you on a medication for the swelling and pain now and following the procedure."

I sank myself into the foam mattress, propping my arms on the rails of the bed. Each individual notion of the thousands that raced to my mind insisted on my attention. Each seemingly speaking louder than the next. So loud that the ongoing conversation between Dr. Hitchman and my parents grew into an incoherent, faint and distant echo. I remained in a daze until my time in the hospital was over and was sitting in the backseat ignoring whatever my parents had to say. Not to be disrespectful, but what words could give any solace at all in a moment of that type of magnitude? We pulled into the driveway and before the car was even fully stopped, I jumped out and ran to my room, slamming the door behind me before thrusting a pillow over my face.

As I lay in my bed, I listen to the sounds of birds chirping outside my bedroom window while the sunlight beams through the blinds and on to my body. I lay there, one small tear falling from my eyes after another, waiting. Waiting for the world to change. Waiting for my world to change. Suddenly I forced myself to stop crying when there was a knock at my door; I began to wipe away my tears with my shirt sleeves, briefly burning my eyes in the process from rubbing too hard.

"Princess can I come in?"

"Come in dad."

Strangely he slowly opened my door as if he were attempting to sneak in. He poked his head around the door, showing only his timid face. Its as if he was unsure of if he should come in, regardless of me saying to. I looked into his eyes from afar and immediately realized from the look on his face why he seemed that way. I knew it all too well. It was the same look that I gave my parents as a child, hell even now, when I wanted to ask them something that I knew that I shouldn't or something that I wasn't sure if I was ready to hear the answer. That "Can my friend spend the night" look.

Finally he walked in and without saying a word he hugged me. Random hugs were always typical in our household, but this time the embrace was just a little bit harder and a few seconds longer. After taking a seat at the end of the bed, we stared at one another, until eventually the awkward silence was broken.

"How are you feeling sweetheart?"

"I'm fine. How are you?"

"I'm great. Thank you for asking " he said jokingly.

I simply smiled in response. Continuing to question what my dad wanted to say.

"Are you scared?" The tone of his voice hinted that he already had the answer.

"You always say that people are only scared when they have something to fear, right?

"Yes I do. But you know what I mean. It's ok. This IS scary. Every part of it I'm sure."

"Which part of it are you asking about dad? Is it the part where the doctor said I might die? I mean I admit that those aren't words you tell a kid. My parents, yes, but not me. Either way though, it's not good news in any way, but I'm not scared. Sad, but not scared. I know where I'm going if I die so I'll be fine. You never know. Maybe Jesus likes volleyball."

" I'm glad you know and don't joke like that. Please. You don't have to worry about anything. We're going to do everything to make sure you are up and running and doing everything that you love. You're a beautiful, smart, amazing, and mature seventeen-year old girl. You're my daughter and I am so proud of you. We're going to get through this. Don't you worry."

"When a doctor basically tells you that the chances of you dying are substantial, your life speeds up. Sometimes, you lose sight of things when that happens. You start thinking about death instead of the life you still have. I know I'm rambling but remember the story of Simeon in the bible. He was ill and basically waiting to die, but the wild thing about it Simeon had something exciting and amazing to look forward to while he was still alive. Honestly it's not even that, it's more so the fact that God promised him that he would love until the day he saw baby Jesus. Guaranteed days. Regardless of a circumstance that is something that anyone wants. I'm not even promised to live until breakfast tomorrow but I've got so much to still live for while we I'm here. Now I mean I'm never going to hold baby Jesus, but I have so much in my life that I love. Even if it's only for the next twenty-four months, twenty-four days, or twenty-four hours. Adventures, dates, more laughs to be had and love to give. So no dad, I'm not scared. And yes dad, I am perfectly fine and I know I will be ok. I'm loved, I have friends and family. I'm not dead yet. I'm a blessed girl. I'm just a bit... unlucky."

A long gaze covered my father's face following my words. He seemed confused. Almost like he didnt recognize me. I wasn't sure at first, but after a minute I knew that my words gave a moment of ease to my father's heart as I could see the worry slip from his facial expression after I spoke. His heavy heart began to lighten with the smile he made while his lips shivered to hold back the tears of contentment in knowing that I was confident and faithful through this disaster of a process. Alas, simultaneously while his heart was being comforted, mine was being tormented because I knew that I wasn't being honest with him. Instead I was only feeding him the words I was sure he desired to hear. The fact of the matter was that I was playing my knowledge of the Bible as a way to shadow the truth. The truth.. Was that I was absolutely, undeniably horrified of dying, and undoubtedly terrified of death. The thought of leaving this world, my family, my friends, and James behind to live without me just encompassed my mind and became the embodiment of my biggest fear. That same fear joined forces with my anger. The anger that stemmed from my wallowing in self-pity which I felt I so rightly deserved.

I drove myself up the wall, scratching my head and repeatedly asking and saying "How could this be happening to me? What had I done to deserve this? I went to church every Sunday and Wednesday. I prayed every night. I talked about Him all the time, at FCA events, with friends, all of it. So is this what I deserve for it? Truly?" On the other hand I thought of all of the things I had done outside of my relationship with God. I was on the track to be Valedictorian. I was going to graduate high school with a high school diploma and an Associate's Degree. My future for school and volleyball was set knowing I was about to be a Clemson Tiger. I felt robbed and that I was robbing others of so much: Myself of continuing a great life, my parents of precious time they didn't have so they could take care of me, my friends of wonderful dates and memories in our last year of high school. My life was so precious and planned out. Now its in ashes and I have no clue how to rise from them. On the surface I might seem like I am handling everything with grace and poise. Though the reality is that I am just a painfully scared little girl.

Chapter 14: Goose

What is our identity? Is it what we view ourselves as or rather how we are viewed by others? Now throw a curveball into that question and add the question of what if we don't really know how we view ourselves? Would the answer therefore be defaulted to the only answer left? Which is it is how others see us. Well I believe that is the answer in my case. One moment, one night changed life in the weirdest of ways.

I went from walking down the halls of the school virtually unnoticed and only being acknowledged through the occasional head of a few people just being polite, to having complete random people stopping to ask when the next party was. The only thing that was more strange was the fact that when people stopped me, they referred to me as Goose. Which I didn't mind. But only one person had ever called me that and only a few people were around when he gave me the nickname. So how is it that twenty plus people are now acting so familiar with a name that I'm only getting used to myself?

Regardless, the sudden recognition from a number of people grew on me like a child's desire to be told they are doing a good job or that someone is proud of them. Each time it happened, I awaited the time it would come again. The gratification I got from a simple name made me feel like a tool. Whether it came from Ashley in my culinary arts class, Shane from the school orchestra when I pass him in the hallway as he hit me in the side with his violin case, or from the countless people who acted as if they've known me for years yet I couldn't discern their face from the hundreds of others in the school. From the simple "Hey Goose" to the recurring question of when the next party was, it was obvious to me that although I had gone to school in this area for twelve years now - leaving all the time in the world for an opinion to be formed of me - my face was now simply associated with a single night and apparently a new single name, Goose.

Now 11:45 hits and the bells of the school sounds to create both music and disturbance to my ears. I walk into the cafeteria to the weird mixed smell of baked chicken and some desert that I believe to be a kind of pie. I stood there in like for a few minutes when I turned my head to the opposite door to see Miranda walking in. Her oversized black joggers with a pink shirt and matching black jacket that she had tied around her waist covered her body in a way that it masked the curves of her body and gave off this subtle yet extremely attractive vibe that reminded me of my celebrity crush Billie Eilish. We locked eyes from across the room as she caught me mesmerizing her very existence. From twenty feet away I could see her blush while she brushed her hair behind her ears and she turned and sat down at a table nearby. Soon after Wyatt, Lilli, and James came inside as well to join her at the table. Simultaneously I was struggling to keep my lunch plate balanced in my hand while the uncanny weight of mashed potatoes were dropped onto it.

After typing in my student identification I saw a hand motioning over from the corner of my eye. There I sat at the lunch table, now accompanied by whom I hoped to be new friends in Miranda, Wyatt, Lilli, James, and another girl named Dawson whom seemed to be with James rather than the group. James got a good one. She was nice. Always adjusting how she sat, which started to bug me, but still nice and funny as hell.

For a while everyone talked one after the other by bringing up something random like how James (who strangely seemed both composed yet under the influence of something, so I'd guess high on something nice) argued that the Umbrella Academy was basically just Codename Kids Next Door with super powers. For a few seconds it almost seemed like a legit argument but then I realized that's insane.

"See I've only seen number one from Kids Next Door as like a grown up, less bitchy, and more badass Caillou or Hey Arnold," I said thinking that I had made a pretty solid comparison.

They laughed as Miranda spoke up asking, "Maddux what the fuck are you talking about?"

I almost went to explain what I said before my conscience replayed the millions of times that people try to explain after a joke and no one is listening so you get a second, "What the fuck are you talking about" or a "my bad I wasn't paying attention" and realize they aren't caring about what you're saying so you feel kind of bad; so I simply decided to not reply and stay quiet.

From that point on we each separated into our own conversations. James and Dawson looked to have a topic on what the better sport was between baseball and volleyball while Wyatt and Lilli debated which of their original hometowns of Oakland and Philadelphia had the better food. Before my conversation with Miranda could really get started, I had a Snapchat from two girls that took me looking at their snap story just to vaguely remember them from my party:

"Hey Goose. A friend of mine gave me your snap and said you might be having a party next weekend or sometime soon? Is it cool if me and some friends come? ;)"

Her head rested on my shoulder as Miranda peeked over to see the message.

"Someone's popular I see."

I laughed out of not knowing how to reply to that.

She asked "So we're throwing a party soon?"

"Oh is that right?

"Yes it is. What are you doing after school?"

"Not a thing."

"Good. Come over and we'll plan."

Now I'm not sure if I'm just very hopeful and a bit certain or just naive, but I feel like planning a party is the least of the interests here. I like it.

Chapter 15: Miranda

I'll be honest, I really did want to plan out a party. It just leads to great pictures for Instagram, a crazy amount of drunk snaps (hopefully none I regret) and just an overall good time. But mostly I figured I would take the time to grow a little bit closer to Maddux. He exuded this confidence while somehow seeming a bit unsure of himself.

He came over to the house to plan things out (even though I told my parents that he was here to study). One after another we threw out ideas. I must say that I was impressed with how much alcohol he planned for. Kegs, beer pong, beer ball, bongzillas, jello shots, some liquor here and there along with hunch punch of course because well... why not? I only chimed in and suggested that maybe some weed be there. I wasn't wanting it for everyone, mainly just our friend group. It was also a different way to asked if he smoked. Come to find out, he most definitely did. We continued talking about the party and the expectations for it. It had to be bigger than the first one. So the more the merrier. We invited countless people to the point where we had to stop and realize that we had not even thought of the venue. How the hell did we skip step one?

I looked out of my window and looked at our RV in the yard. Immediately I thought of the boat landing that was located nearby the RV park that we go to about half an hour away. The summer had ended and we were in the midst of autumn so the place was usually vacant this time of year as it was typically not a big thing to go do at this time of the year. The boat landing happened to be just enough space to fit all of the cars possible along with hundreds of people. About a half mile from any main roads and surrounded by trees seemed to be as perfect a spot as any.

However, there was the issue that it was public property and there wasn't any lighting in the area. It being public meant no fires could be started. However, at a certain time of night, I highly doubt it matters. Then there are the police. It's pretty much known that around here if there is a chance that you could get a ticket, then you are most likely going home with a ticket. There was a time that the Sherriff pulled over his son and wrote him a ticket; he made him pay every last dime of it and take the course to keep points off of his license. So if he will do that to his son, what do you think he would do to a bunch of kids partying at a boat landing, underage drinking, doing drugs and probably throwing trash down every other square foot of a place that is pretty much in the backwoods? I guess we would find out.

"Maddux, how do you feel about having the party at the boat landing?"

"The one a few miles from the park?"

" Yes. "

"That works for me."

Now there it was. Basically all planned out with us sitting and working out the rest of the details, constantly getting sidetracked by music, or Netflix shows until he was there for about six hours, which was absolutely insane considering my my parents are the type to threaten to take away your door if you close it with a bit over. He walked in my home as a new friend. He walked out as something even more than a crush. Maddux became a regular at our house. Honestly it never dawned on me until the questions from Lilli and my parents shifted from "Is Maddux coming over," to " What time is Maddux coming over, or are you two going out somewhere?" My friends became his friends as he went out to do things with us. He came along for all of the late night dirt road riding, countless beer pong tournaments that he continually stunk in. I mean really stunk. Had I met him while he was playing beer pong, we would not be friends. But away from the table he was the most amazing thing I knew.

He kept me smiling when I was stressed out. We FaceTimed each other until we were both snoring on our screens. As cliché as it sounds we never had to say goodbye because it felt like there was a certainty to us that we would see each other later on. He had a way of taking whatever problem it was and minimizing it to the smallest degree and showing me why I have no reason to worry about it. He helped me be happy and I only hope I did the same. We saw each other in the hallways at school and flirted the same as any couple that had been dating for half the year would do. The difference however, was it had been a few weeks. It was so Disney channel insta-lovey that I almost felt uneasy about how quickly things were picking up. At the same time, I wouldn't have changed a thing.

Infatuation. Temptation. The thin line where these two words meet became the space that I stood on every single time that I was around Maddux. That line only seemed to increasingly stretch thinner when we were alone. Like the first time we had sex at my house while everyone was running errands. The way our bodies touched and minds connected immediately aroused me. Every touch sent electricity through my veins. My breaths deepened, making me gasp for air as my hands gripped the sheets and pulled him tighter with my legs. It left me insatiable and craving more of that feeling. Our once innocent days together now consisted of hanging out, dates, and salivating in the dopamine rush of every satisfying sexual encounter that followed.

Our relationship grew like a new tooth. At first you might not be able to see it, but eventually it is as clear as day, and very permanent.

It was amazing. You remember the stories that you hear of individuals finding each other, only to have things go south? Well that couldn't be more opposite than he and I. It was marvelous. We spent evenings tasting countless ice cream at Cold Stone or strolling along the beachside feeling the wind blow and listening to the waves crash onto the shoreline. Then there were the more peaceful nights together where we spent most of our time laughing than actually talking. When we did speak, it was effortless. We ran through subjects like a mad game of Jeopardy. We discussed our favorite Netflix shows and debated which animated movies were the best by putting them in a bracket. Him choosing Ratatouille over A Bug's Life might possibly have been the only time he truly upset me. Although some nights we skipped the jokes and stayed up spilling over our emotions.

It wasn't as if he was buying me countless things or spoiling me on dates. He just gave me his time. His presence. It was as though being in his presence transcended the absence of Brad. Whatever void I felt from Brad being away was immediately filled with another memory made with Maddux.

So much so that it seemed like memories began to overlap. It all started when I checked the mail and saw a letter from Brad and where I used to run to my room to rip open the envelope, I now simply threw it on the table in t he living room. However, from that second on, every time that Maddux came over or we were out together I would have deja vu after small things that were said such as when he mentioned music he liked and talked about that artist the same way that Brad used to. My attraction grew non-stop but there were more so a couple of yield signs in those deja vu moments; so much so that I felt like I had to mention Brad in some fashion to Maddux in order to get it to go away.

We sat on the swing sets at the park nearby my house. Mind you, that same swing set we had made our official spot just days earlier, so it carried a little sentimental value each and every time we went there and even magnified memories from before.

As we swung back and forth, trash talking as to who could swing the highest, thoughts of this strange love triangle surfaces to the forefront of my mind. Then I quickly realized that that triangle existed only to me. Both Maddux and Brad were truly numb to the others existence. I put my feet down so that the top of my shoes stuttered along the ground to slow me down until I was stopped. Maddux, who was then bragging on what he assumed was a victory - which it wasn't - started to stop swinging once he saw what he called my "Doctor Doofenshmirtz face" whenever I was in deep thought. Which was also a small jab at my pointy nose.

"What's wrong?"

"I think I should tell you something," I said lowly.

"What are you pregnant? Actually have a boyfriend and he wants to catch these hands? Saved fifteen percent with Geico?"

I debated back and forth in my head of whether to talk about it or just keep my mouth shut. Then I looked at him to see him staring at me like a puppy with bright eyes and waiting for me to talk. I caved.

"How do you feel about long distance relationships?"

The randomness of the questioned lingered in Goose's mind before actually resonating with him.

"I feel like there's a right and wrong answer here and I'm not sure which is which. But if I'm being honest, I hate them. I don't know I just want to be able to physically touch and embrace who I'm with. If not all the time, at least a considerable about of time."

He reached his hand out to grab mine while interlocking their fingers to hold hands. Looking her in the eyes he said, "This. This right here is a lot of what I need. If I don't have this or can't do at least this when it's really needed, then I don't think I can do it. Not to knock the people who can. I'm just not one of them. Why are you asking though?"

"I used to be one of those people who thought they could handle being that kind of relationship. He was in the Air Force and

I was..well me. The relationship was great in itself though. We were together for seven months. Everything was amazing. We spent what felt like every minute of the summer together except for about a week or so when he had to go to his family's event at the same time I had my family reunion out of state. We talked all of the time and everything was just how I wanted. That is until he told me that he would be leaving for basic training in Texas at the end of the summer. I always knew it would be coming up, but I guess I just never accepted it. Fast forward and he left. So I'm here alone. Going through days without my best friend. No one to tell my problems to at that exact moment other than Lilli and it's just not the same because Lilli is a real "suck it up and keep moving" kind of sibling, whereas I'm the opposite. The days felt isolated and the nights grew lonely. I feel like the more alone I felt, the further I was away from him, even though I know the love was still there. I just grew apart until it was as if he wasn't in sight and I decided for myself that it was over. But now here I am, with you, and I don't think I could be happier."

My words soaked in Goose's head. It seemed as though they gave him a pleasant satisfaction meanwhile inevitably questioning whether that happiness is only because of presence. He was curious, but there was a strange gratification in believing the latter and just saying that I was happy with him and would be anyway regardless of the circumstance. Sometimes the fear of our reaction to discovering the truth of reality is all it takes for to turn a blind eye to something we feel is a red flag waving in the distance.

Chapter 16

Bottom of the twelfth, tie ball game at three a piece, and a runner at third base with one out. It was another wild game of MLB between Wyatt and James. The two of them looked intensely at the screen. James was the home team felt comfortable with his chances. Wyatt seemed just as confident since James basically swing at everything.

As soon as Wyatt chose his pitch, James sent the runner from third, and squared around to bunt. A perfectly placed bunt was laid down the third base line.

"Pick up the ball! Pick it up," Wyatt screamed while mashing every button on the controller.

Four to three. Game over. Wyatt threw his controller on the ground.

"Let's run it back," teased James .

"Nah fuck that game. I've gotta figure out what I'm wearing tonight for the party."

"What party?"

"Seriously? Goose and Miranda's? The boat landing? Where the hell have been? "

"I don't remember hearing anything about when the party was, just that there was one."

"Bro, why do you think Lilli and your girl are at the mall shopping for stuff right now?"

James shrugged his shoulders. "Hell if I know."

"Well they're getting outfits for tonight. Then once they get back we're getting ready and going to Lilli's house to pregame and then head out."

"Oh I got you. Man I'm not gonna lie, those two are pretty good together."

Wyatt snarled, rolling his eyes. "Nah bro, she's fucked up. Me and Lilli were talking about it and she said she doesn't even think she ever broke up with Brad. The one that left for the military."

"Deadass?"

"Dead ass serious. That's why I can't fuck with it man. That's messed up."

James asked, "Well hell what is she going to do whenever he comes home?"

Before Wyatt could answer, the door opened with Dawson and Lilli coming through. Soon after, the four of them hopped in the Wyatt's truck and were off. Excitement and a couple shots of vodka had all of them hyped for the night. The drive to Lilli and Miranda's was only about thirty minutes but regardless, James was still like a small child when it came to car rides. No matter how hyped up or motivated he was, as soon as his head tilted to the side on Dawson's shoulder, he was out like a light.

Chapter 17: James

Our pain. Our demons. Our troubles and frustrations of life. Are they meant for us to face alone? Most people would argue that they aren't. But to those people I ask them this. If my demons aren't for me to face all alone, then why do they only haunt me? Why do those voices decide to set up camp in the deepest parts of my brain instead of choosing to attack you as well? Do they call you by name like you have been friends with them for years? Do they bring up memories of your past as if they were present for them as they twist the narration of those events in such a way that you begin to let tears flow from your eyes from the mental turmoil they instill along with the strange physical pain of your chest caving in as the feelings of air pushing down on your lungs like a cardboard compactor increases until the air around you ceases to exist.

Then in those moments you start to hyperventilate. Fighting for air as you drown on dry land. The thoughts that haunt you lay back as you struggle because they know what you do too; that the same thing you are wanting so bad is literally all around you. The air you are wanting is everywhere yet there is something disconnecting you from receiving it, so you continue to panick. Then this last until your mind finally shuts down and the voices and thoughts that exhaust you decide to leave you alone. The troubles of life leave you alone. The spontaneous unknown worry that has no face or description finally leaves you alone and you can breathe again.

Now let's take these deadly horrors and confine them to a seven foot by seven foot box. A space that while I sat inside of it my senses were concurrently evicted from therein. My ears were subdued to a silence that at first seemed hardly bearable. Meanwhile, my eyes had been redirected to the aphotic zone as my sense of touch vacated my body, causing it to suspend in mid-air. It was warm, dark, and forlorn. The only thing that seemed to work in my body was my mind. Thoughts of the past like the joys of winning a title game and jumping into my dad's arms after the final out, followed by the agony of watching tears fall from my mother's face at funerals were just a couple that manifest itself to pull at my heart. Every high and low and all that is in between was felt with every fiber of my being during that time. For what felt like hours, my mind lined up all of my emotions and fired the starter pistol for them to ignite at once.

I soon went from floating, to crashing to the bottom of the box as it began to spin slowly until completely stopping. The top and bottom remained completely blackened as well as the walls in front and behind me. This left only two sides, both of which were now completely clear like glass walls. To my left, a highlight reel was revealed. The once quiet room now echoed the voice in my head that narrated every thought that came.

The highlight reel began to play. There he was. It was a thinner version of him than I could remember. It was a familiar place as I could quickly tell that we were outside of our home. Beside him was a bucket of baseballs that I could distinguish as such from the Diamond logo on it. As I looked closer, I saw a small head and shoulders peeking out in the space between my dad and the pine tree that stood tall on the side of the house. Instantly I realized that I was seeing myself at just two years old, holding a small bat and crying my heart out. The memory that I was being shown became clearer when it panned over to the door to my mother barging out to tell my dad to stop. Like a movie you've seen a million times, I quoted my father's answer before he ever said it.

"Go back in the house. If he wants to learn how to play, he's going to have to learn how to play the game the right way."

And that's exactly what happened. Because from that moment I was shown the fast forwarded clip of me learning how to turn on pitches so that it hits my backside while I cried, and continuously asked when I could hit. It was funny to look back at and remember, especially when I remembered how horrible I thought that day was at the time.

The highlight switched to him sitting on the bleachers beside my mom during a game that must have been just years ago as I looked fairly similar to the way I do now. I walked up to them after the game and my mom stopped us and wanted to take a picture. She snapped the picture but for some reason the entire highlight stopped and seemingly screenshot itself as it turned into a single Polaroid picture. Then a rush of memories came up and each of them turned into pictures from that moment until the side of the box was filled. I took a second to look and saw moments from the time I was two years old up until the day he died.

Abruptly all of the pictures lit on fire. They burned, but the box did not become hot. So there I stood watching those pictures burn, yet never turn into ash. Instead, what should have been the ashes actually started to form together as the pictures were now made into a scrapbook of memories. Each picture was in it. Each moment was recorded. Every memorable laugh, every heartache, every big moment. It was all there. That was until that side of the box grew dark and into that darkness, the scrapbook faded away.

Soon after there was a clip that was presented to the clear space to my right. The once transparent side changed to a view of me sitting and talking. As the viewpoint panned out from behind me it started show a headstone over my shoulder. The headstone read James A. Taylor (which I knew was not me because we had the same name yet different birthdays). February 12, 1965 - February 12, 2014.

I was just sitting their spilling over countless things. I was just talking to my father's grave with the belief that he was right there. For a brief moment, it was a strange and somewhat ghost-like or holographic version of him was sitting on top of his headstone, smiling as big as always, looking ever so attentive to every word I said. Both of us had this glow in our eyes that said "I wish you were here."

The closer I looked, the clearer things became such as me noticing that I kept flipping through pages of something whenever I talked.

Eventually the sun started to set and a voice said softly, "It's time to go sweetheart. We can come back again anytime." That soft and caring voice was that of my mother. The heart and glue that held the entire family together while I sulked. She was there for me. Alongside her stood my love and my dearest friends in Dawson, Miranda, Goose, Wyatt and Lilli.

I stood up and closed the pages. To my surprise I was holding the exact same scrapbook from the previous highlight reel. I turned around to an immediate group hug. The embrace was heartwarming and mind-easing all the same. Then all of the heads turned towards me. But not the image of me that I was viewing, the actual me that was sitting trapped in the box. Each of them reached out their hand. I stared at them for a second with a subtle smirk. I stuck my arm out and as soon as I did, my arm went through the side of the box like a portal. Instantly I felt like I was being pulled through until my entire body had come through.

I gasped for air as I jolted out of my sleep. My sudden movement and sound scared everyone in the vehicle. It was only a dream. It took a few seconds for me to calm my breathing, yet once I did I was at peace. The memory of my dad reigned in my head, but the gratitude for the people who were still here was magnified in that moment.

"Hey, are you ok?" Dawson asked.

I smiled, kissed her on the forehead and replied, "Perfectly fine."

We continued the ride until finally arriving at Lilli and Miranda's house where it seemed that Goose had already beaten us there. It was party night, but that would not stop us from pregaming and having a few drinks while watching a movie and playing some games. It was set to be a long night, but I'm glad it was with these people.

Chapter 18

James looked through the window for a second when he spotted a black camaro speeding down the street. At the same time Lilli looked up after hearing the revving of an engine not too far away and saw the same car. James locked eyes with Lilli, motioning his heads towards the window as if to say "Who is that?"

"Oh no," Lilli whispered while she tapped Wyatt on the leg as James did the same to Dawson.

"I think I'm about to get something out of the truck and start putting our stuff up," James said.

Immediately James opened the front door to the camaro sitting in the driveway and a guy with blonde hair and sunglasses sitting there playing music; the bass vibrating the ground below, muzzling the words of the song.

Not a single word was needed for the rest of the group to simultaneously get up from their seats.

"We're about to go ahead and start throwing everything in the truck too," Wyatt said.

Miranda looked puzzled as she replied, "There's literally twenty minutes left."

"This movie is pretty much over. Plus everyone here knows that the rich dude from the first movie is behind all of it."

"Thanks for spoiling the movie. "

"We're just packing regardless, and you've seen this a thousand times. We're about to get ready." Dawson interrupted.

"Sure I guess so, " Goose mumbled.

As everyone walked away, Goose and Miranda sat on the couch, surrounded by nothing more than the sounds of the airplane scene of the movie blaring from the entertainment system. As it became increasingly clear that neither was watching the movie any longer, Goose reached on the table to grab the remote. As soon as he moved it, he saw an envelope with Miranda's name on it.

"What's this?"

Miranda's face began to sink in when she realized he had picked up her letter from Brad.

"It's nothing."

"Well it's got to be something. It's from Texas. So I'm guessing it must be kind of important being the fact that Dallas isn't necessarily a few miles away."

"Maddux it's nothing."

"Wait a second, Texas? This is from that dude isn't it? Y'all still talk?"

"No we don't. I got that like two weeks ago and as you can see I haven't even opened it. So chill out."

"I'm fine I'm just trying to figure out what he wants. Just take a look," he said while turning the envelope over to her to grab.

"It's not even worth it. I don't care what it says."

"Or maybe you don't want to see what it says while I'm here."

"Are you serious right now?"

Miranda turned her head trying to sell Goose on the notion that she was annoyed when the reality was that he was spot on with what was said.

"Maddux I told you that I was done with that. Yes, I would be lying to you if I said he doesn't at least come to mind every now and then or whatever. But it's never anything I'm stuck on. He's off in Texas and I hope everything is great with the Air Force and I'm happy for him, but his safety and things are as far as my thoughts of him go and maybe occasionally of how things might be if he didn't leave."

"Then why the hell are you still here if you're thinking about somebody else?"

"Because I'm over him and what we had. Because you're here. You're here with me Maddux! We're here, together. I've spent all of this time with you and for what? I've confided in you and told you about things for what? Gone out with you and tried to be the best I can for you. For what? Because I want you. Ok? I love you."

They both stopped. The blood rushing through their veins as they popped out of their skin and their hearts pounding with such ferocity that you could almost see them ready to take a leap out of their chests.

Then Goose rushed in, grabbing Miranda by the waist to pull her closer. He gazed for a second with his hand on her face, his thumb brushing over her cheek and said "Me too."

In the kiss that followed Miranda wrapped her arms around his neck, yet almost simultaneously letting a single subtle tear fall down her cheek as it rolled down the outline of her jaw until dropping onto her shoe. Then leaning back to brush her eye with her shoulder sleeve for it to go unnoticed. Her heart began to ache as if small strings within it were slowly tearing apart one by one. That emotion reigned so genuine because although it was a kiss in a moment so intense, so passionate, so sincere on his part, she could almost feel her heart debate on whether to finally completely shift from Brad as its key holder to Maddux. Meanwhile, the thoughts of how terrible of a person she was haunted her troubled mind due to the fact that she never ended anything with Brad, but rather only began to distance herself knowing that he would have no way to know why. She hadn't even opened the last letter and had almost forgotten it. As for Goose - even though her feelings for him were genuine - was horrible in letting things get this far, or anywhere for that matter, without telling him the full truth. More damning thoughts began to shovel their way into her mind as she realized when she said to him "Because you're here," he must have thought she meant because he was here fighting for this unfortunate circumstantial relationship that on the surface was very much real and worth it. Sadly, she knew that she failed to finish the rest of the phrase which would have ended in "and Brad isn't." A name that Goose even up to this point has never even heard come out of Miranda's mouth.

A few seconds later Lilli walked by struggling to carry what looked like her entire life completely and impressively stuffed into a duffle bag.

She stared at the both of them with a look of disappointment before saying, "You two might want to stop kissing. There's someone outside that I'm sure you both probably would like to talk to."

Wyatt walked by soon after, patting Goose on the back while letting out a sigh.

Goose followed behind to open the door to allow Miranda to pass through. The butterflies from the moment before still remained with her, growing by the second. That was until she stepped outside and saw whom everyone else had already spotted. She stood there frozen as that emotion ceased immediately. Her heart began to twist into knots and her chest felt as if it were spartan kicked into oblivion. Behind her, Goose stood there as happy as he could be. Yet in front of both of them stood the only thing that could throw a wrench in this situation.

"Hey babygirl," he said.

"Brad, what are you doing here?"

"You didn't see my letter? I told you that I would be coming home to you soon. But I see you guys are going on a trip."

"Just a party tonight. You should come!"

As soon as those words left her lips she thought to herself "How stupid can you seriously be right now?"

"That would be perfect," he said while walking towards her, and embracing her in his arms.

"Who's this," Brad asked while stepping back, quickly looking at Goose.

Miranda could feel herself sinking through the ground, drowning in thoughts of if they somehow would both say something about being her boyfriend or if they would both spill over and say everything else that she had failed to do. So she spoke up to intervene.

"This is Maddux, but a lot of people call him Goose."

Brad looked at Goose as if he were questioning what he was just told. "Goose? What's up I'm Maverick," he said while reaching out for a handshake.

"Oh dear God no. Don't. His name is Brad. Only Brad," she interrupted while subconsciously wishing they would stop acknowledging the others presence.

Brad looked up, laughing before saying "Been keeping my girl out of trouble or too busy keeping yourself out while she gets you all into it?"

"Your girl?" Goose questioned.

Quickly all of the attention shifted to Miranda.

"Is this the dude you were talking about?"

"Aww you talked about me while I was gone? That's nice," he said jokingly.

Left speechless, Goose walked away to the truck.

Everyone else watched from a distance as the situation slowly unraveled. Mouthing their opinions to themselves before turning away. From that second it became clear that this night was being set up for a whirlwind of emotions.

Chapter 19

Each of them stepped out of the truck one by one. The only conversation coming from what seemed to be the only couple that was enjoying themselves in Wyatt and Lilli. They joked while Lilli teased him of the numerous wins she had over him in UNO. The only slightly heated moment coming from the reactions that followed as Wyatt came back with the comments of how she was childish for thinking that you could add draw two cards on top of draw four cards.

"In what world can you put a few two on a draw four" he yelled.

Lilli replied "Any world with people who have common sense knows that you can do that!"

"No you can't" he exclaimed with his arms motioning to every word which for some odd reason seemed to make him more convincing.

"Yes you can. You know what, I'll just look it up now."

Never in the history of the world has someone typed a question so quickly into Google.

"UNO confirms that you are not allowed to stack draw two and draw four cards."

A look of sheer disbelief washed over Lilli's face.

"This is bullshit, you just suck at UNO. No one plays like that!"

Wyatt laughed, only amused at the fact that his point has been proven. The back and forth between the two was like a light that floated amongst the group in what felt had grown into a darkening evening.

They all sat around the fire; the skin on their hands cracking as the blood began to flow through their cold hands to warm them. Everyone remained silent, none unwilling to break the obvious tension, yet each having something to say to at least one other member of the group. They all grew increasingly uncomfortable with every second that passed and slightly embarrassed of every eerie moment of accidentally locking eyes at another.

"Can someone just please say what they want so we aren't just sitting here with our dicks in our hands?" Goose said.

They all began to laugh. That small comment seemed to break every wall of tension that surrounded them, except Miranda. Because she knew that as nonchalant as it may have been said, it was a small jab at the silence that had been created between she and him since they got in the car to make the trip. At least that's the only thought that her mind could calculate.

"Maddux, can we talk for a minute?" said Miranda.

Goose sighed. His eyes rolling to the back of his head as he sat up and walked towards the dock. Brad sat back, confused while watching the two of them escape into the distance. He looked at the rest of the group , sure that they had some clue of the situation at hand. "What the hell is going on?"

In the distance, Miranda pulled the sleeve of Goose's denim jacket. He yanked his arm away and looked at her, both enraged and broken.

"I didn't know he was going to be here! I didn't mean for this to happen."

"Are you serious? Miranda it doesn't matter whether you meant to. It only matters what you did and didn't do."

"Maddux.."

"No let's just take a look. You didn't tell me that this dude even existed or that you were in a relationship. You didn't tell me that I was just a holding place while he was gone. Hell I can tell he has no idea. So you didn't tell him a thing. But what you did do, was spend your days with me and your nights confiding in me about your daily issues. But mostly, what you did was look me in the eyes and say that you love me knowing that you sent a message to him saying the same thing."

"I do love you."

Goose put his hand up, signaling for her to stop.

"Do me a favor please. Don't ever tell someone that you love them if you know that there is someone out there that you love more. Because I don't think there is any worse feeling than to be held up on a pedestal, only to realize that it has second place written on it. No one deserves that."

"You told him you love him?" a voice said softly in the distance.

She froze while her brain simulated her doing a 180 degree turn to face the voice head on. Ashamed with her eyes buried into the dirt she mumbled, "Brad."

There the three of them stood with animosity brewing by the seconds. Goose and Brad stared at each other in a way that seemed as though they were telepathically unveiling everything that has gone on in Brad's absence.

Brad turned to look at Miranda, ill-faced and hurt and put his arm around her shoulder, gently using his hand to lean her towards him while barely resting his head on hers.

"Goose right?" he questioned.

"My name is Maddux."

"Well Maddux, thanks for taking care of my girl while I was gone."

"Yea well I guess it goes without saying that she'll have to find someone else to take care of her when you leave again."

They both fixed their eyes on Miranda once again. Her eyes sunk and chest tightened as she felt the weight of the world slowly push her down. She couldn't dare look up at either of them. The only desire she had in the moment was for the Earth to swallow her whole until the situation had eroded and it was safe to be seen.

"Right. She will need someone else when I leave."

Almost simultaneously they turned away from her. Heads down, hoods overhead, hands stuffed into their jackets, and walked away.

Chapter 20

With tensions boiling over between the three of them, another situation was coming to its head just feet away. For the entire time, James and Dawson sat around the fire, hand in hand, completely silent. However the feeling was of an enjoyable silence but rather an unfortunate loss for words.

"Did I do something?" Dawson asked.

"No. It was just a long ride up here and I'm just a bit tired."

"You're lying. You slept most of the ride other than when you jumped out of your seat and scared the hell out of me. So what's the deal? Was it the dream during the ride? You haven't acted the same since."

James just slowly turned to her, caressing her face before softly kissing her on the forehead and turning back to the fire.

"It was your dream. Wasn't it? Just tell me and stop trying to hide whatever is going on. You should know by now that I'm here for you and that you can talk to me about whatever it is."

She begged and pleaded for him to give her an answer. Some kind of answer. Just any answer at all. It wasn't until she uttered the words "I love you" that finally became the last bit of pressure that burst the pipes causing a frustrated and silently grieving James to cave in.

"You wanna know the biggest lie that I was ever told?"

"What." she said while resting her head on his shoulders, her arms clinched around his arm while holding his hand tightly in both of hers.

"It was one that I told myself ironically. You know I always used to think to myself 'I've got time.' But that's not true at all. Because you see I don't have time. We don't have time. Time has us. We are the sand in the hourglass, not the one who turns the hourglass over. We always laugh and joke about killing time. I guess in a way that's true. We're all just killing time, until time kills us. "

"Let me ask you something" James said with a look of anguish.

Dawson, immediately snapping out of her attempt to process his words replied. "Yes?"

"Is it worse to have the opportunity to give someone you love a proper 'I love you' before they die and not take advantage of it, or for them to die and you never have the opportunity to tell them "I love you" one last time in any form?"

Dawson stood there speechless. Her eyebrows raised and eyes started to survey the situation.

"It was the night before his birthday. I was at the pre-season opener for my baseball season. My dad was in the hospital awaiting his surgery that would change things to how they used to be. At this point he had been sick for about four years. Neurosarcoidosis. I don't know much about it other than what the internet could tell me. From what I read its like a complication of sarcoidosis. It caused inflammation in different parts of the nervous system. I'm not sure. It's just Wikipedia. Anyway, this surgery was supposed to fix something in his neck that was going to change things for the better somehow. Unfortunately he got a strange fever that wouldn't go away in the days leading up to it. I didn't think much of it because I mean what's a fever to what he's been dealing with. Fast forward to that night and I ended up going 0 for 4 in the game. I was irrate. I didn't want to speak or have anything to do with anyone. So I get home and get a call from my dad. For some reason he just seemed so happy. We talked and he asked how my day had been and how the game went. I told him 0 for 4 and he just persisted to know more. Which I should've known, he always cared about the 'how' and not the 'what' of situations. Of course I told him four line-outs. Then it was like I could see the smile on his face through the phone when he told me 'You'll be fine. Don't worry about it. Just keep swinging and they'll fall. They always do. It'll work out. Just keep your head up son. ' But I was such a selfish little prick that I wasn't trying to hear any of it. At the time I was almost hell bent on sulking in the results of the game. That stupid sulking cost me. We talked a bit longer and then he said 'I love you son!' But I was such a brat - so selfish - that I shrugged it off saying 'Love you too' just as low-toned, quick and non-affectionate as possible while releasing a huge sigh which almost drowned out the words. It was the kind of low pitched answer you receive from the most shy kid in class when their name is called upon by the teacher to answer and the kid knows everyone is looking. It was shameful. The disappointment in his heart could be felt in his tone when he told me to give the phone to my mom. I could feel him choking up trying not to let me hear his silent sigh on the other end of the phone; but he told me to give the phone to mom, so I did. Come to find out, those would be the last words I ever said to him. He died the very next morning, at 8:00 a.m. on February 12, 2014. His birthday. Sepsis. My mom didn't go super in depth with me on what exactly happened other than they believe that the sepsis caused his heart to fail or it created a blood clot in his lungs. I don't know. "

James stopped for a moment, choking up on his words while he fought back the tears. He started to rock back and forth, putting his face in his hands to make his motioned to wipe his watery eyes more indistinct.

He sat back up and sighed.

"Wednesday, February 19, 2014, the day we buried dad. Granted I went and questioned a lot in the week that led to his funeral, but it wasn't until that day, that my mind started to become what it is now. I'm not sure what switched but I was the only one who didn't shed a tear that day. I had buried it. I held that pain, anger, confusion, all of it in because I knew it wasn't going to make anything better at all. That was the day I finally came to the realization that crying won't change the half-assed "I love you" I said to him that will forever be the final words I said to him. So I went into that day, and everyday that followed with an emotional mask. I taught myself to smile when I wanted to cry. Laugh when

I wanted to scream. Console others when I was in need of help, and simply lie by saying "Yea I'm fine." I put that mask on everyday, for as long as I required myself to (which was anytime I was in the presence of someone else), until the very second I could get alone to myself and break down. Then that routine became a part of me and how I dealt with everything. I stored everything in so that I could - by everyone's advice - keep moving forward. Physically I made all the growth possible. Mentally I never left the graveyard. School? Most definitely not. Mainly in the sense that I can't focus on a single thing. I can sit in a lecture and be attentive and then, boom! All of these thoughts come to my brain and seemingly take me out of the room. I sit there, in a desk, but my mind is far from the place. There isn't a single place to escape it, so many days I lay in bed and don't move a muscle. I want to sleep all day because my mind keeps me up all night. Sometimes I'm up for days. I find a few things to take my mind off of it but I know my troubles are never far away. So then I worry. Don't get me wrong though, I do have fun and have genuine smile and laughs. "

James paused. His pain stricken eyes began to fixate on hers. He moved his hand to caress her face, gently brushing her hair behind her ear. Then the silence took over. Dawson's face grew red as she blushed and her infectious smile emerged. He pulled her closer, resting his forehead on hers.

"Then there was you" he said. "You've come into my life and have honestly been so amazing. In such a short time you've become someone that I know I want in my life forever, no matter what. One look into your eyes, a second of hearing your laugh, or a glimpse of your smile erases the worry from my mind and keeps me locked in whatever that moment is with you. I know I messed up the opportunity to tell my dad this the right way but I refuse to miss the opportunity with you, because I don't know what tomorrow brings for either of us. So I want to tell you now, face to face, that you mean the world to me Dawson Montgomery. You're a blessing, and I love you. "

Dawson looked on, soaking up every word. As she processed everything. Her smiled became uncontrollable.

"James, your dad loves you so much. I never got the chance to meet him but I'm sure he wouldn't want you living in pain like this. He'd want you to go be happy and live your life. Remember him, love him, but be okay in knowing you'll see him again someday. I know it's gotta be hard. I don't know what I'd do if I lost my dad. You're strong just for handling this. But you don't have to be strong all by yourself. Not anymore. I'm not sure that I could at this point. Why didn't you tell me this sooner? I'm your girlfriend. I'd sure like to know something like that James. I could've helped somehow or at least just been there for you."

A dull ache engulfed James's heart the second she finished speaking. Not one of pain, but the kind of ache you get after a weight has been lifted. The kind of ache that lets you know that pressure and weight used to be there but it no longer remains. Amongst that small relief that spawned his current subtle heartache, Dawson still continued to comfort James with her encouraging words. He gathered himself once more saying "You were already there for me. Just without knowing. Maybe I could've told you. Maybe so. But I wasn't ready to and I just couldn't do that to you. "

"Why not? Do what?"

"Because you have enough pain to deal with of your own than to have to walk around knowing I'm in pain also. You're too caring, too loving, too selfless. If there is such a thing. I figured that the second you heard that I'm anything but happy, you'd do all that you could to fix it."

"I'm not sure why that's a bad thing? "

"Because the way I saw it, you'd spend all this time trying to fix my problem. I don't think you realize that after you deal with someone else's pain for so long, its like it partly becomes your own. Not in a literal sense, but figuratively. Because you would do everything possible to share that burden to lighten the load of the other. Yes, you might accomplish that. So from one side of the equation you did an amazing thing right? But what about the other side of it? From that side all you did was add on to your own shoulders. You just compiled it with your own worries. I couldn't bare to do that to you."

"I'm sorry but that's an insane way of thinking. I'm here, and I'm going to stay here. Nothing you go through from now on will be alone. Let me be what you need in those moments. I'm just asking for you to please not shut me out about stuff like that, or anything anymore."

"Ok. I won't."

"Promise me, James."

"I promise."

Instantly James's curiosity peaked.

"Umm ok what is it?"

"There are umm...tumors on my spine. They weren't too big at first, but now they're pushing down on my spinal cord. I found out weeks ago and we were going to take some medicine to try to limit them and the pain but that doesn't help at all. My legs get numb after a while. Sometimes they tingle, or I'll have this insane back pain that just makes me want to cry."

Although she'd never actually said anything to James about it, he hoped she didn't think of him so displaced that he didn't notice when she has to slightly moved to her side and discreetly stretch when she's been sitting down for a while. Does she not understand that he recognized the fear in her voice when he offered to pop her back and she declines? Even the times that she gingerly walked liked she had worked out legs for three days straight holds her lower back the way you see pregnant women do. Plus it didn't help that Dawson absolutely refused to tell James what's really wrong. It's just hard for James to believe that it's just sore or a strain from volleyball yet watch her sit on the bench while it's public knowledge that she's going to Clemson. Suddenly it all made sense.

"Why wouldn't you tell me about this," James asked.

"I don't know. I was scared I guess."

"Scared of what?"

"Scared that you wouldn't want to be with me or continue everything that we have if you knew that there was a chance that I could be paralyzed."

He scratched his head, tilting it to the side and said, "Paralyzed? What are you talking about?"

"Because they press on my spinal cord, that's very possible that it could damage it to the point of paralysis. I know you don't want to deal with that."

A sadness and nervousness shadowed over her while she put her head down, running her feet through the dirt.

"Babe, I will handle whatever we need to. You're worried about my reaction to something that in no way changes how I feel."

"Yea but it would," she yelled.

James motioned his hands to tell her to calm down and spoke softly, "No it would not. You see my mom always told me that the only physical traits about someone hat you should fall in love with, are their smile and their eyes. Because those are the only two things, that will never change. The rest of the body will grow old and wrinkly, fat or skinny, but those eyes and smile are forever the same. Dawson your hazel eyes and infectious smile are the only physical things I really care about. I mean don't get me wrong the rest of you is just, I mean have you looked in the mirror? But I'm not worried about any of that. I do worry about it for you because I know what it means to you. But no matter what happens, I will be right here with you. Every single step of the way and never leaving your side."

Her lips started to quiver as butterflies floated around in her stomach.

"Sounds like a smart woman. I'd love to meet her. But honestly I'm just so scared. One minute I was doing everything I wanted and the next, I'm just hoping everything works out where I can still walk. That's not fair. Then they put me on this medicine that isn't doing a damn thing to help and it hurts worse every single day. This morning while I was out with Lilli I had to step aside and call my dad. They called Dr. Hitchman and they set up the date for the surgery to be Tuesday. On my birthday. Yay."

"I'll be here for you. I'll make sure to send you a message and hopefully you won't be knocked out for too long after and I'll make my way up to the hospital."

"Yea. Just hoping they don't literally kill me trying to play around with my spine. That would suck," she joked.

"I know you're joking, but please don't say that."

Chapter 21

For the next hour, the caravan of headlights scintillated through the trees. Teens flooded the area to the point that seemingly every grain of sand and blade of grass was covered. Each time you looked up you were treated with the incredible yet misunderstood image of wild adolescence.

If you looked by the trucks near the entrance you could see blunts being passed in rotation like clockwork. A few of them choosing to eat gummy worm edibles but making it very clear these weren't to share when shouting "these are not gummy worms!"

If you looked closer to the inside of the cars parked beside them you'd find the group snorting cocaine off of the center console and bumps from their keys. Which was especially odd due to the fact that they were parked close enough to the fire that it illuminated parts of their faces for a clear sight at the key being raised to their nostrils.

Once again beer pong remained a staple at the party because at anytime of the night that you looked, it was being played by the same two people who were sifting through opponents and winning games like there were scouts in attendance.

Turn your head a little more and you catch a small glimpse of everything. You'll notice the endless camera flashes recording people shotgunning beer or even Four Lokos before throwing the cans on the ground when trash cans were only feet away . At the same time you can't help but admire the mob of people dancing and singing with their cup held high and spirits even higher.

It was a fun, beautiful, relaxing, incredible night whose only purpose was to appease to the wonders of drinks, drugs, and debauchery.

However for the faithful group of friends, it was spent overseeing the forsaking of each other's idiosyncrasies; none more obvious than Miranda and Goose.

Miranda, the infamous life of the party, had now been reduced into a ball of tears and shots of tequila sitting on the tailgate and leisurely passing along through the crowds of people.

Goose on the other hand, fully embraced the wild scene. He drank as if he had an immunity to alcohol poisoning. Then after many failed efforts to stop him, he consumed drugs at a rate that his body trembled from not being able to discern whether to be mellowed from the indica strained weed or to move a hundred miles and hour from the cocaine. The most peculiar sight of the night was Goose playing beer pong and winning . The winning wasn't strange, but rather who his partner was. Goose and Brad? No one was sure whether they were genuinely clicking as friends or merely puppeteering Miranda's mind after catching her stares from the distance.

Wyatt spotted Goose stumbling off into the distance before taking a seat on the ground. It wasn't until that moment that he decided to intervene. He waltzed through the see of bodies to get to his friend.

"Goose! What's up, man? Umm honestly I was originally going to let you drink your frustrations tonight, but after seeing you fail like right sobriety tests just trying to get here on the ground, I figured it was about time for you to chill a bit. "

Goose laughed and looked up to Wyatt while motioning his hands like a jack-in-the-box to reveal a big middle finger to him.

They shared a laugh that lasted a few seconds longer than felt comfortable. Wyatt simply turn to Goose and finally asked, "Are you ok? Seriously?"

"Do you ever wonder why some people have such a hard time with love? Like perhaps it's the conflict between knowing whether it's something that you give or receive, not realizing that it is both." Goose said while tossing sticks into the woods .

Wyatt laughed. "Did you just say perhaps? Ok I see you. What do you mean?"

"So many people spend their time giving their whole hearts. They give every ounce of love that is in their body to a person. They become their shoulder to cry on, their shield when they are scared, the laugh when they are down, the smile that keeps them going, and they would give them every star in the sky if it were possible. They give everything, while the other person does nothing but receive all of that love. You see the issue comes because a lot of times we give our love to someone who doesn't know how to give it back. They're like vampires when they feast for blood. They just take all of your love until you're drained of it and then move on to the next. Now after that happens (in the eyes of some), when you're left with no more love to give, how else do you gain that love again but to drain someone else the same way it was done to you? Some intentionally, others habitually because it's all that they know. Then it becomes a cycle of heartbreak, until some genuine, strong, brave soul comes along and refuses to allow someone to ruin them, and they take what's left of their own love and leave before it's too late. They leave and share it with another precious soul that reveals to them that true love is a joyful endless journey, and not a dark one way street with a dead end. We need more good people like that in this world. I need that. I don't know who hurt Miranda, man. From what she said about him, it couldn't have been Brad. So who? Why? Why would she waste all of that time with me, knowing all I wanted was her? Why hurt me when I did nothing? Maybe someone deserved it, but not me. Not by her."

"I'm sorry bro. I know that shit has to be horrible. "

"I don't know. It seems like it took me forever just to finally be with someone who makes me feel like myself. The guy who creates hardcore debates about what animated movies are best. It's *The Lion King* in case you didn't know. I'm one of the first people you pick for pickup games but also one that you wouldn't expect to play the shit out of a violin or bake some crazy stuff. I'm basically Zeke from High School Musical. I'm a lot of things. Miranda just happens to be the only one who knows all of me. I don't know. I want to go after her, but at the same time I'm not so sure that's a good idea. It's like she's running away, yet standing right in front of me at the same time. "

"Listen, I could be wrong, but from what you just said I view the same as when you chase someone you want to be with. I don't know much about love but unfortunately I do know about love lost. Bro, let me tell you something. One... Don't ever chase someone. Two... If by some dumb reason you decide to, then just make sure you don't ever get into a relationship with whoever you had to chase. Because when someone is being chased, it means they have no desire to be caught. So even if you do somehow catch them, they won't stay still for long, because their intentions weren't to stop running."

On the other side of the landing, Lilli walked over to her sister who was sitting alone on the back of a tailgate, clearly sobbing and eating peanut M&Ms. Lilli stood in front of her and stared with a scowl.

"You look angry," Miranda said.

"Who? Me? No. I'm just trying to figure out where the hell you got those M&Ms, " Lilli replied.

"They're yours, yes. I just wanted some comfort food."

"Comfort for what?"

"Have you not been paying attention to what happened with Maddux and Brad?"

Lilli sighed and shook her head.

"I've seen everything."

"Then you understand why I need comfort food right now."

"Actually no I don't. But I understand why you deserve to be slapped in the face."

"Excuse me?" Miranda asked while dropping her M&Ms from her mouth.

"How are you seriously sitting there and acting like you're the victim in any of this?"

"Because I.."

"I don't care, " Lilli interrupted. "I don't care why you think you are because the fact is that you played those dudes. You don't care about them."

"That's not true! I love him," Miranda cried.

Lilli chuckled, "Who is him?"

Miranda paused. Because for a moment she realized that she didn't even know the answer.

The rest of the night was spent with Goose and Brad doing everything they could to avoid Miranda. Somehow it's like they managed to always end up on the complete other side of where she was. Although they never said a word to one another again for the night, they routinely locked eyes with her. First Goose, then Brad. Never for longer than comfortable, but always long enough to feel the disappointment.

Chapter 22: Dawson

Tuesday, November 7, 2017. It is five in the morning and my alarm sounds, but I laid in bed already awake. In fact I hadn't gotten much more than a half an hour of sleep the entire night. For hours my eyes never left my phone screen. I scrolled through the endless pictures and videos. I found it crazy how so many memories were condensed into snapshots and ten second Snapchats. No wonder my phone constantly alerted me that my storage was full. I watched and admired everything I was able to see. Each video from pregame bus rides, every post-game picture with teammates and friends, and even the videos of my training that I used to have watching. I missed sharing the court with my team. As crazy as it sounds, I missed being at practice and having Coach Roberts call me out on each and every mistake. It was like a part of my identity was being taken away when I realized there was no way that I would be able to play with tumors. It was depressing honestly.

But as I lay there - now scrolling through Twitter for memes - my phone vibrated with a text from James flashing across my screen:

Good morning baby! ⬜ I know it's early and that you have to be at
The hospital soon but I just wanted to say Happy Birthday! You are
absolutely amazing and I don't know what I'd do without you. You
will never understand how much you truly mean to me. But I promise
I'll do all that I can to show you. I know you may be scared about
surgery, but I'm praying for you and everything will be ok. I'm sure
that you'll be asleep and resting for a good while after surgery. Just
message me whenever you can babygirl. I'll make sure to come by
when you're awake. I love you.

The brisk breeze from my ceiling fan circulated throughout the room along with the air condition that my mom religiously sets at sixty eight to cover my entire body with chill bumps. I began typing back when a spasm caused me to drop my phone gracefully on to my face and then fall on the floor. I shivered, clinching my comforter to my body. A slight numbness overwhelmed my body. It started with my back pulsating as I lied in my back and tried to count the rotations of the fan. The sensation increased, leading me to turn over to my side, grabbing a pillow to put between my legs because I heard it helped with spine alignment. Perhaps that was simply advertisement because the pillow did nothing for pain. My medication was out of the question because of surgery.

Moments later my parents walked in to wake me up to see my lying in pain. They helped me up and get ready, which made me a bit uncomfortable because I kept over thinking the fact that it seemed unreal that they could have to do that all the time. Dad picked up my phone and put it into my bag as mom walked with me to the car. In exactly two and a half hours, I would be under anesthesia, asleep for hours with no control on what happens.

After arriving I was given a wheelchair and was pushed to almost straight to the recovery room as we went through each precaution and test needed beforehand. After a while, the nurse provided me with my gown and eventually I was in bed anxiously awaiting Dr. Hitchman's arrival. My distress had not subsided. I began to nibble at my fingernails from anticipation an occasionally sighed so loud it was only comparable to a child trying to notify that they are bored or need something. I needed this surgery to begin and this pain to be dealt with.

Soon after Dr. Hitchman came in. Following about a two minute pep talk I felt at ease. His confidence flowed throughout everyone in the room. His presence seemed to lift the team. Just the feeling that they pushed that they cared about my well-being meant to world to me in that moment.

I said a final prayer before they put the mask over my nose and mouth and ordered me to begin counting down from one hundred. I had never been under anesthesia before but I had a feeling that it would more like be more like falling asleep.

"100... 99... 98... 97... 96... 95."

Instead I was met with a completely different experience. The prickling that radiated through my legs was now vacant. The palpitating of my muscles that exhausted my lower back had now ceased.

"89... 88... 87... 86... 85"

My eyes became weary and my mind foggy. But not before grasping what had happened as a last single thought rushed to my mind before slipping into unconsciousness.

"I can't feel my legs."

Happy birthday to me.

Chapter 23: James

Time with her went by like a sunset. Beautiful, peaceful, yet never lasting quite as long as hoped. But to every sunset comes another sunrise and there is no better description of her than that.

Her good morning texts filled with bible verses and hearts were like the violet and blue rays that begin to shine over the morning sky at twilight. It was a glow and inspiration to my day that signified to me her saying "I'm here" and no matter what happens, there is light in this day and you can find it with me. Next, it was her voice that melted my heart like the warm orange that blended into the sky as the sun peaks its head over the horizon. So gentle, so sweet that it was both my motivator and my support. It was the voice I heard at the beginning of my day telling me to get up and go, and the voice that chimed in to say "keep going."

Then the moment where the sun has completely been lifted into the morning sky finally comes along; while it boasts shades of red that form the violet lining along the atmosphere with white clouds faded throughout as birds take flight to a new day. For myself, that graceful and remarkable vision could only be seen when I looked into her hazel eyes and admired her gorgeous smile. She was the epitome of majesty and elegance. It was that quality about her that still commanded my attention just as it did that very first day in the auditorium.

She was the love of my life. It takes a certain type of person to be able to love you so much that they love enough for the both of you. She seemed to be this angel of mine; so strong, with a soul that encapsulated the very definition of incredible. Call it fortunate. Call it lucky. I call it a blessing to have her.

It was about six-thirty in the afternoon and basically the entire day had gone by without hearing from her. Obviously I wasn't expecting to here from her before the evening because of surgery but as the clock ticked by I grew questionable as to if everything had gone well. If there's one thing that Dawson always did, it was text me back. Slowly but surely small doubts that there could be something wrong started to creep in. I had to make sure and decided to get to the hospital and see her. So my already lead foot grew a little heavier on the gas. Then even more substantial.

The speedometer quickly started leaning further to the right. Sixty, seventy, then eighty miles an hour. Then my phone began to ring. Pastor Montgomery's name shown across my screen. I reached down to the cup holder to grab my phone, mindlessly taking my eyes off of the road whilst still pushing my foot into the gas pedal.

"Hey Pastor Montgomery. How are you doing? How's Daw.."

A horn sounded, prompting me to look up for a moment. At that second the lights of an eighteen wheeler bounced from every angle of glass in my car and blinded me. I grabbed the wheel and jerked it to the right. In an instance, I was looking at the road from the view of my sunroof. The sounds of metal bending and glass shattering along the roadside vibrated my eardrums. The doors of my once very spacious vehicle now crumpled around me like cheap scrap metal in a compactor. My neck jerked forward towards the steering wheel, then off to the side before being snapped back by the airbag that deployed and seatbelt tightened in front of me, leaving me glued into the seat. Broken glass flew across my body as it sliced my arms and face. I continued to roll until my car turned over and stopped into a ditch. Even while only lasting about fifteen seconds, I've never felt more helpless and afraid as I laid there bloody and battered, breathing heavily as I clung to life with all that I had until the pain shut my eyes.

Chapter 24: James

There I laid in a hospital bed, seemingly hooked up to every machine they could manage to attach to any free space on my body. My entire body ached as I noticed the cuts and bruises that covered my skin. There was a small fan raised by the television that had a cold breeze that blew just hard enough to make me want to crawl back under the blanket. I scanned the room and saw my mom in a deep sleep on the recliner beside me. Lilli and Miranda were on their phones snapchatting; which I could only tell because of that single filter that distorts your face and gives you this sometimes annoying but generally hilarious squeaky voice. Then I look up I hear the heated debate between Wyatt and Goose about whether LeBron was ever going to win a title in Los Angeles.

Almost everyone was there for me, yet I still wondered how Dawson was doing and if she still had full function of her legs. The racing thoughts exhausted me until I rested my head back down on the pillow. Following was a light knock on the door and then the screech of it cracking open.

"You should really be more careful when you drive."

I lifted my head as Miranda and Maddux step to the side. My eyes grew wide and a smile came upon my face.

"Hey baby."

"Hi."

To be continued...

Part 2 - May 2020

In Honor of

Cleveland McNealy (Grandfather)

James Taylor (Father)

Annie McNealy (Grandmother)

Sheletha McNealy-Williams (Aunt)

You are forever loved and missed!

Made in the USA
Columbia, SC
03 April 2020